Designing Houses
An Illustrated Guide

by Les Walker and Jeff Milstein

The Overlook Press
Woodstock, New York

First edition 1976
Published by
The Overlook Press
Lewis Hollow Road
Woodstock, New York 12498
Copyright © 1976 Les Walker and Jeff Milstein

ISBN 0 - 87951 - 035 - 8
Library of Congress
Catalog Card Number: 75 - 7684

We dedicate this book to everybody who
had a positive influence on our lives:
parents, grandparents, friends, and rela-
tives. The following people have been
particularly inspiring:

Bob Anderson
Hobart D. Betts
Joan Beveredge
Richard Bouchard
Barrie Briscoe
Marvin Buchanan
The second-year architecture students
    at CCNY
Sandy Connors
Deborah Franke
Marty Garbus
Keith Godard
Mr. Good
Craig Hodgetts
Al Lees
Sandy Lipshutz
Robert Mangurian
Peter Mayer
Scotty Mitchell
Charles Moore
Eli Nivin
Tim Prentice
Robert K. Robison
Miss Schaum
Gabe Silverman
James Stirling
Roz Streifer
Robert Venturi
Jess Walker
Joan Walker
John Wasylyk
Peter Wilson
Bernard Zimmerman

Table of Contents

Introduction 6

Meeting Fred and Lois and 9
Their Family

Setting Up Your Office 10
The Complete Office 12
The Minimal Office 13
Dress 14
Tools of the Trade 15
Buying Your Tools 15
Using Your Tools 17

Gathering Information 26
Looking 28
Recording Visual 30
Information
Photography 30
Drawing 32
Keeping a Notebook 36
Dreams 37

Designing 38
Site Drawing 40
Program 44
Bubble Diagrams 47
Design Principles 54
Ventilation 55
Climate 56
Space 58
Movement 59
Shape 60
Combined Shapes 61
Light 62
Defining Shape 63
The Plan 64
Symbols 65
Kitchen Planning 66
Bathroom Planning 67
Stairs 68
Furniture Cutouts 69

Sketches 71
Study Models 72
Final Plan 86
Finish Models 88

Preparing Construction 90
Drawings
What Construction Draw-
ings Are 92
Beginning 98
Gather Information 98
Give Yourself a Crash
Course in Building
Construction 99
Learn Some Structur-
al Principles 112
Set Up Your Tools 115
Lay Out the Sheets 116
Drawing 117
Symbols 118
Draw Your Design 120
Dimensioning 122
Show the Size of
House 123
Locate Walls, Doors
& Windows 123
Labeling 125
Describe Doors, Win-
dows & Other Im-
portant Parts 126
Specify Siding, Roof-
ing & Other Impor-
tant Materials 128

Titles 130
Codes & Permits 144
Building Codes 144
Building Permit 144
Your Seal 144
Construction Contracts
and Supervision 145

Appendix 148

OH FRED,
JUST TO THINK
WE DESIGNED
IT OURSELVES!

Introduction
Be Your Own Architect

Being practicing architects, we continue to find many people who want to build a house for between $10,000 and $40,000. But not just any house. They want a home that reflects their personality and is economical to build and run. They don't want to live in a trailer or a development, or to use a standard builder's plan. The average architect's fee for the design of a $25,000 house is $4,000.00, so before ground is even broken, a large chunk of their available funds are gone and the many people who want to build on their own often wind up with a home they never wanted.

Architects are professionals who have studied and trained hard. It takes a great deal of energy and experience to develop a set of plans that makes a client happy. Architects rightfully like to get paid for this. One of the most time-consuming aspects of the architect's job is to devise a complete program of the client's needs. This program, if well done, will lead to a shape that fits the new owner's style of living. Form follows function—the architect must define function before he starts giving form. He must become well acquainted with his client so that he knows his/her style of living. The more personal the program, the more livable the building.

However, no one can outline a more personal program about the client's style of living than the client. In his head are all his dreams and the life experiences which make him unique. So, the hard part is done. What he needs now is to learn a few basic skills and tricks to design a home that fits his own uniqueness.

DO ALL THESE PEOPLE LIVE THE SAME WAY?

This book, then, is a step-by-step, how-to-design-your-house guide for people who want to save an architect's costs or for those who simply want to create a more personal plan than an architect might design. And it is written for those people who want to learn what an architect does. We have attempted to write and illustrate the book to allow for each reader's personal taste.

In the back of our minds was always the thought that it's fun to design your own home and that there is a special pleasure to living in a home you have designed yourself.

ONCE UPON A TIME THERE WAS A LONG THIN SNAKE WHO LIVED IN A LONG THIN HOUSE

HE MARRIED A SHORT FAT SOW WHO LIVED IN A SHORT FAT HOUSE

THE LONG THIN SNAKE COULD NOT GET COMFORTABLE IN THE SHORT FAT SOW'S SHORT FAT HOUSE

THE SHORT FAT SOW COULD NOT GO THROUGH THE DOORWAY OF THE LONG THIN SNAKE'S LONG THIN HOUSE

SO THEY READ A BOOK ON DESIGNING HOUSES

AND THEY REDESIGNED THEIR HOUSES. THE SHORT FAT SOW AND THE LONG THIN SNAKE LIVED TOGETHER HAPPILY EVER AFTER

As a starting point meet Fred and Lois Sample and their children. We invented them to provide a model of how a family with no previous architectural background might go about designing their own house following our step-by-step directions and their common sense.

We'll follow Fred and Lois and their kids throughout the book; at the end, you should be able to look back and see how their needs, their land, and their pocketbook dictated the final shape of their house.

Jess **Phoebe** **Fred** **Lois** **Lincoln**

1. Setting Up Your Office

The very first thing you will need is a place to work, or your "architect's office."

It will be the center of activity for everything that relates to the design and the drawing of your house.

In this chapter, we'll show you how to set up an office to fit your energy and budget. We'll introduce you to a group of simple tools you'll need and like using. We'll show you how you should dress (with tongue in cheek). In short, follow the lessons here and you'll be ready to open up your "practice."

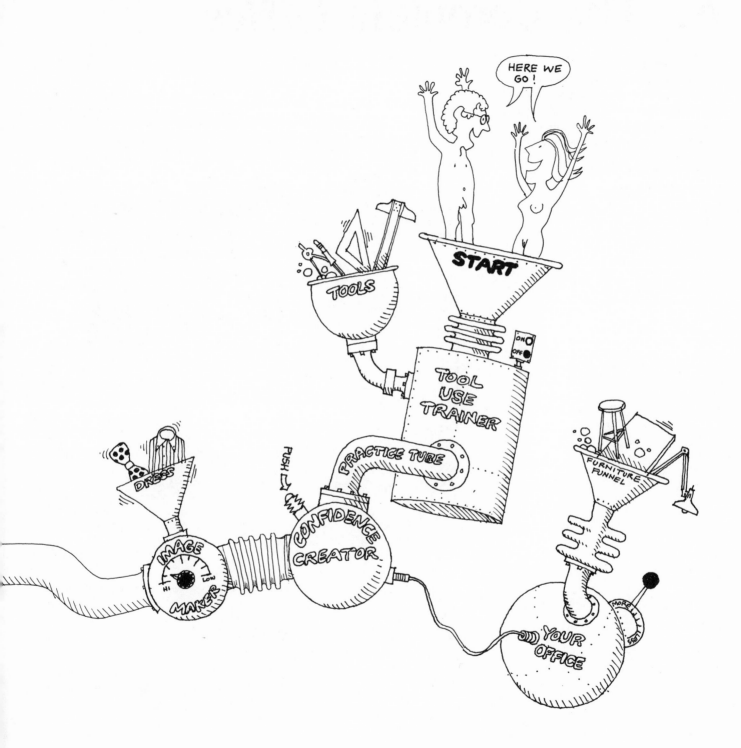

A. The Complete Office

Here is a simple way of setting up a pleasant, well-lighted, well-ordered place to work that will organize all the little tools and papers that otherwise might cause an incomprehensible mess. All the materials are available from your local lumber yard with the exception of the architect's lamp which can be bought at a drafting supply store.

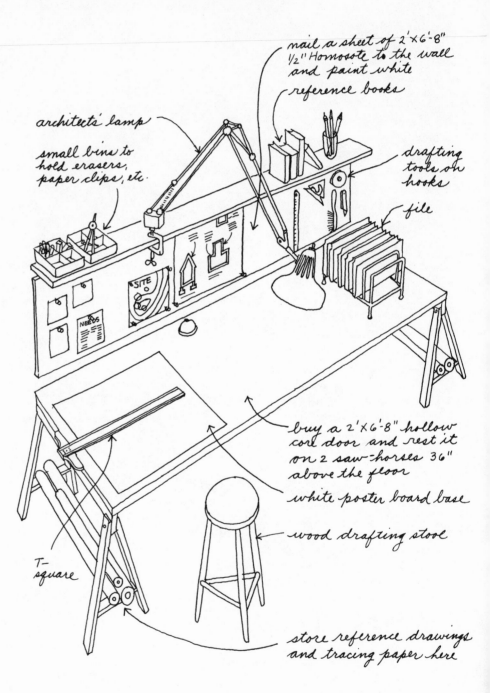

nail a sheet of 2'×6'-8" ½" Homosote to the wall and paint white

reference books

architects' lamp

small bins to hold erasers, paper clips, etc.

drafting tools on hooks

file

SITE

NEEDS

buy a 2'×6'-8" hollow core door and rest it on 2 saw-horses 36" above the floor

white poster board base

wood drafting stool

T-square

store reference drawings and tracing paper here

B. The Minimal Office

If you're on a really low budget and/or cramped for space you might want to devise a minimal setup by using the kitchen table with a portable tool box. Try to set up near some clear wall space so you can tape up reference information.

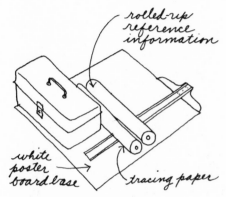

rolled-up reference information

white poster board base

tracing paper

OFFICE IN STORAGE

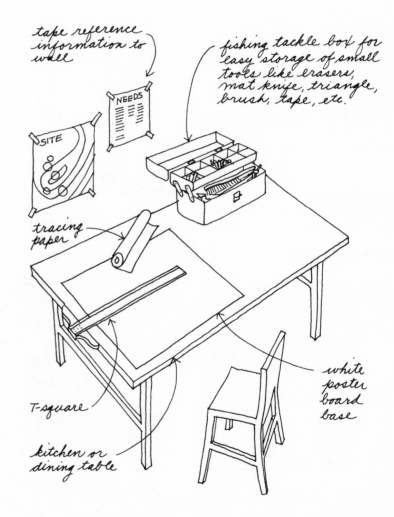

tape reference information to wall

fishing tackle box for easy storage of small tools like erasers, mat knife, triangle, brush, tape, etc.

NEEDS

SITE

tracing paper

T-square

kitchen or dining table

white poster board base

C. Dress

If you're one of those people whose psychology is affected by what you wear, we offer you a few tips on how to architectize yourself. If you're going to be an architect you might as well do it with style.

D. Tools of the Trade

Here is a minimum list of instruments, or tools, necessary for your work. You should poke around drafting supply stores to get good deals on new or used equipment, and to gain knowledge about use. Most of these tools come in several varieties of quality and price. Pick the ones that fit your budget.

The Charrette Company will send you a catalog for mail order equipment. (See appendix.)

1. Buying Your Tools

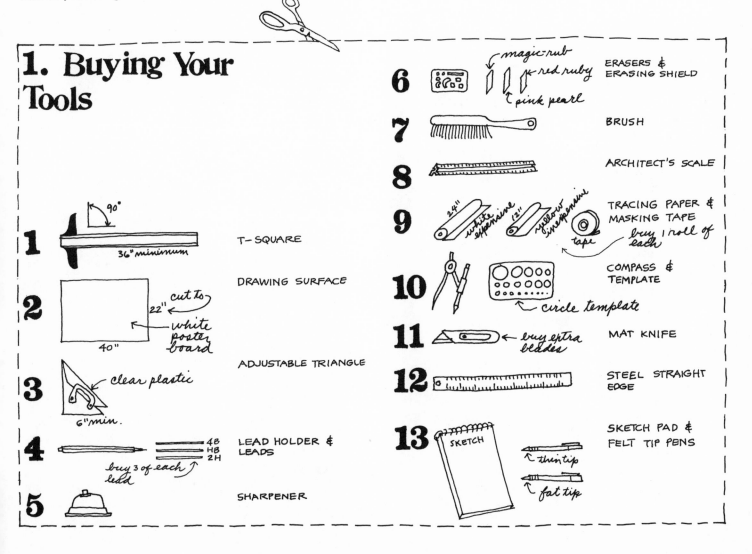

1. T-SQUARE — 90° — 36" minimum
2. DRAWING SURFACE — cut to 22" × 40" white poster board
3. ADJUSTABLE TRIANGLE — clear plastic — 6" min.
4. LEAD HOLDER & LEADS — 4B HB 2H — buy 3 of each lead
5. SHARPENER
6. ERASERS & ERASING SHIELD — magic-rub, red ruby, pink pearl
7. BRUSH
8. ARCHITECT'S SCALE
9. TRACING PAPER & MASKING TAPE — 24" white expensive, 12" yellow inexpensive — tape — buy 1 roll of each
10. COMPASS & TEMPLATE — circle template
11. MAT KNIFE — buy extra blades
12. STEEL STRAIGHT EDGE
13. SKETCH PAD & FELT TIP PENS — SKETCH — thin tip — fat tip

2. Using Your Tools

Beginning on this page is a brief description of how to use all the tools on your shopping list.

drawing board & T-square

Before you do any work, cover the drawing area (the desk if you are using the complete office and the board if you're using the minimal office) with a sheet of thin white poster board. This will produce a bright, clean, smooth surface on which to draw, and will keep the wood (desk or board) from getting dented by your pencil.

If you have a little extra money, buy a more convenient tool for drawing horizontal, parallel lines, called a parallel rule or parallel edge. Most architects use this in place of the T-square.

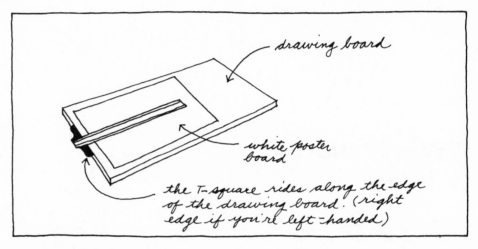

drawing board

white poster board

the T-square rides along the edge of the drawing board. (right edge if you're left-handed)

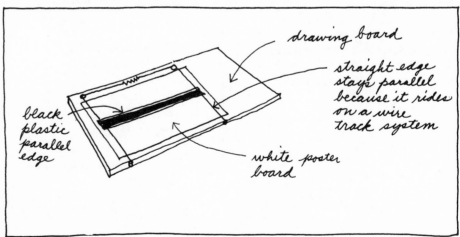

drawing board

straight edge stays parallel because it rides on a wire track system

black plastic parallel edge

white poster board

adjustable triangle

This clear-plastic tool has an adjustable leg that allows you to draw lines that are at any angle.

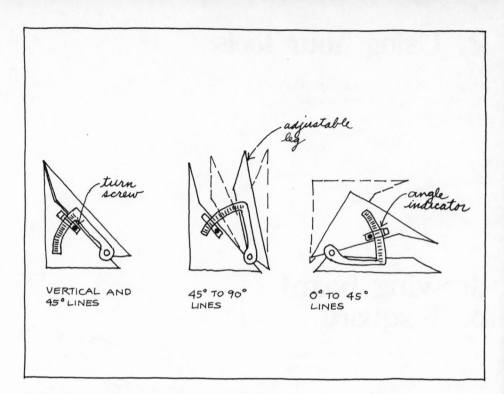

turn screw

adjustable leg

angle indicator

VERTICAL AND 45° LINES

45° TO 90° LINES

0° TO 45° LINES

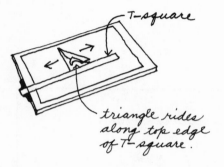

T-square

triangle rides along top edge of T-square.

lead holders & leads

Architects use mechanical pencils that consist of a lead holder, or handle, and the lead, or graphite.

This system is good because many different leads, ranging from hard to soft, can be used in one holder, and the leads can be quickly sharpened.

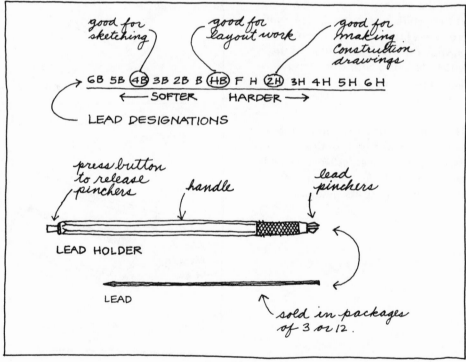

good for sketching

good for layout work

good for making construction drawings

6B 5B 4B 3B 2B B HB F H 2H 3H 4H 5H 6H

← SOFTER   HARDER →

LEAD DESIGNATIONS

press button to release pinchers

handle

lead pinchers

LEAD HOLDER

LEAD

sold in packages of 3 or 12.

sharpeners

You'll need a special sharpener for lead holders. They are designed so that you can sharpen quickly, which is necessary when you need to draw many fine lines in succession.

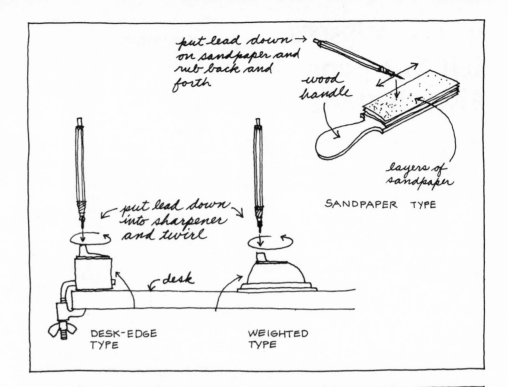

put lead down → on sandpaper and rub back and forth

wood handle

layers of sandpaper

SANDPAPER TYPE

put lead down into sharpener and twirl

desk

DESK-EDGE TYPE

WEIGHTED TYPE

compass & templates

You will need the compass to draw large circles and a circle template to draw small circles. There are many templates available for drawing bathroom and kitchen fixtures, and many different symbols to use, but the only one you'll really need is the circle template.

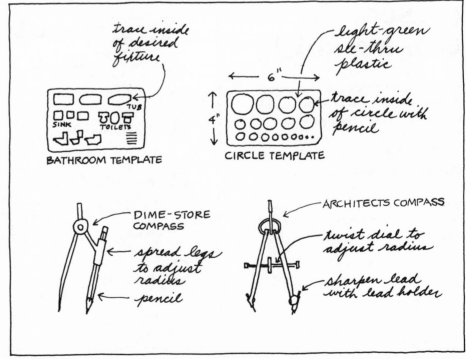

trace inside of desired fixture

TUB

SINK

TOILETS

BATHROOM TEMPLATE

light-green see-thru plastic

6"

4"

trace inside of circle with pencil

CIRCLE TEMPLATE

DIME-STORE COMPASS

spread legs to adjust radius

pencil

ARCHITECTS COMPASS

twist dial to adjust radius

sharpen lead with lead holder

glue, scissors, felt tip pens & sketch pads

Some other tools for model-making and drawings are glue, scissors, felt tip pens, and sketch pads. You'll probably need a fine line and a thick line felt tip pen for various kinds of sketching.

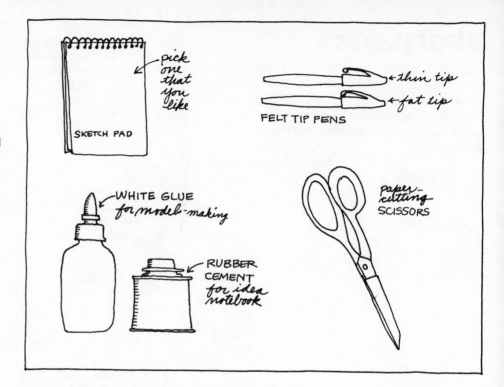

erasers & erasing shield

An erasing shield is a thin perforated sheet of metal that is used to limit the area being erased. The perforation is placed over the area to be erased while the metal sheet shields the rest.

Mistakes and changes causing erasures are an inevitable part of the architect's work. So, you may have to conquer a bit of frustration when you have to erase a lot.

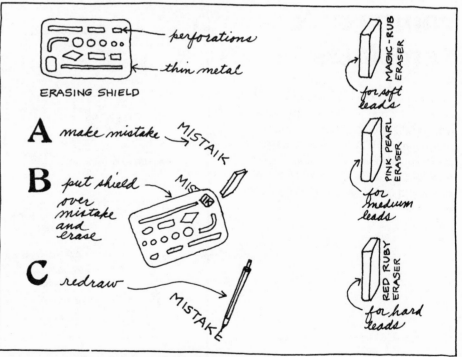

sharpeners

You'll need a special sharpener for lead holders. They are designed so that you can sharpen quickly, which is necessary when you need to draw many fine lines in succession.

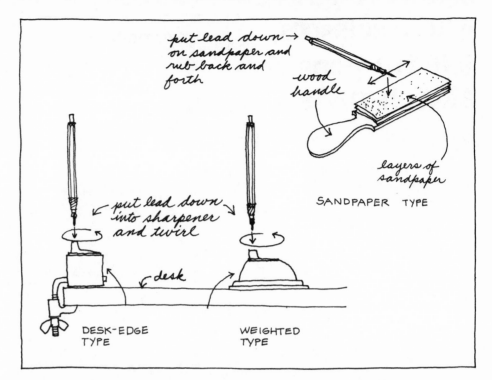

compass & templates

You will need the compass to draw large circles and a circle template to draw small circles. There are many templates available for drawing bathroom and kitchen fixtures, and many different symbols to use, but the only one you'll really need is the circle template.

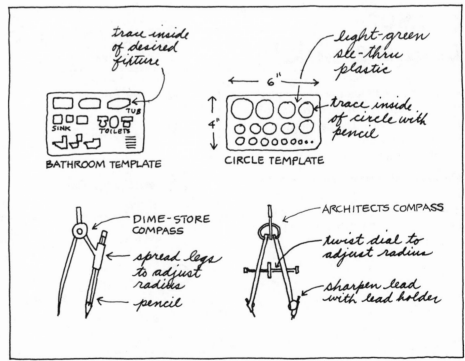

19

glue, scissors, felt tip pens & sketch pads

Some other tools for model-making and drawings are glue, scissors, felt tip pens, and sketch pads. You'll probably need a fine line and a thick line felt tip pen for various kinds of sketching.

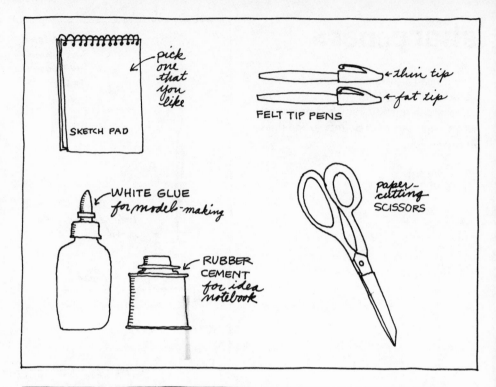

erasers & erasing shield

An erasing shield is a thin perforated sheet of metal that is used to limit the area being erased. The perforation is placed over the area to be erased while the metal sheet shields the rest.

Mistakes and changes causing erasures are an inevitable part of the architect's work. So, you may have to conquer a bit of frustration when you have to erase a lot.

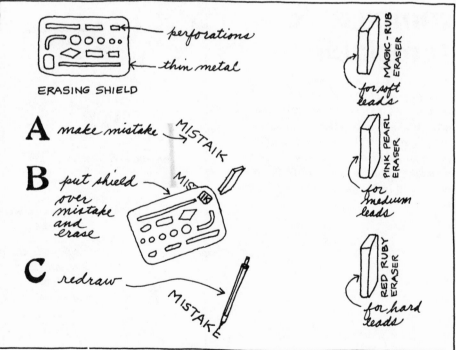

brush

You'll need a brush to remove eraser shavings from the drawing without smudging the remaining lines.

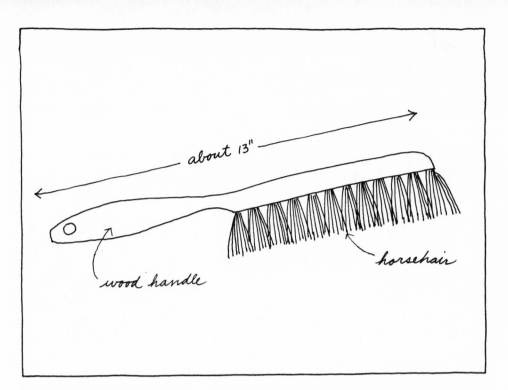

about 13"

wood handle

horsehair

paper & tape

You'll need two types of paper for your work. The first is a roll of very inexpensive thin yellow tracing tissue, often called yellow buff or canary paper, essential for sketching ideas. The second is a good quality heavy white tracing paper for final drawings.

Masking or drafting tape is used to hold the paper to the drawing board without damaging the paper.

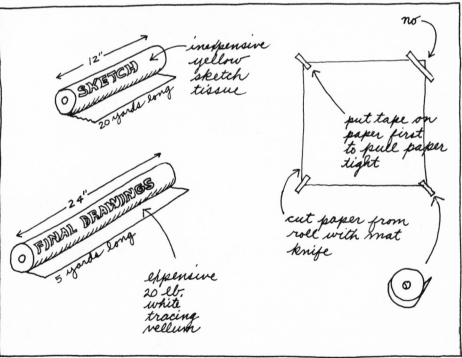

12"

SKETCH

20 yards long

inexpensive yellow sketch tissue

24"

FINAL DRAWINGS

5 yards long

expensive 20 lb. white tracing vellum

no

put tape on paper first to pull paper tight

cut paper from roll with mat knife

mat knife &
straight edge

The mat knife and steel straight edge are instruments that can be used for cutting the tracing paper accurately, but they are primarily model-making tools. Since you will be using cardboard as the principle material for models, the steel straight edge and mat knife make excellent tools for getting clean, accurate cuts not possible with scissors.

Get extra blades because they dull quickly, and you'll need a poster board cutting surface under the material you're cutting to get a clean edge and to protect your desk.

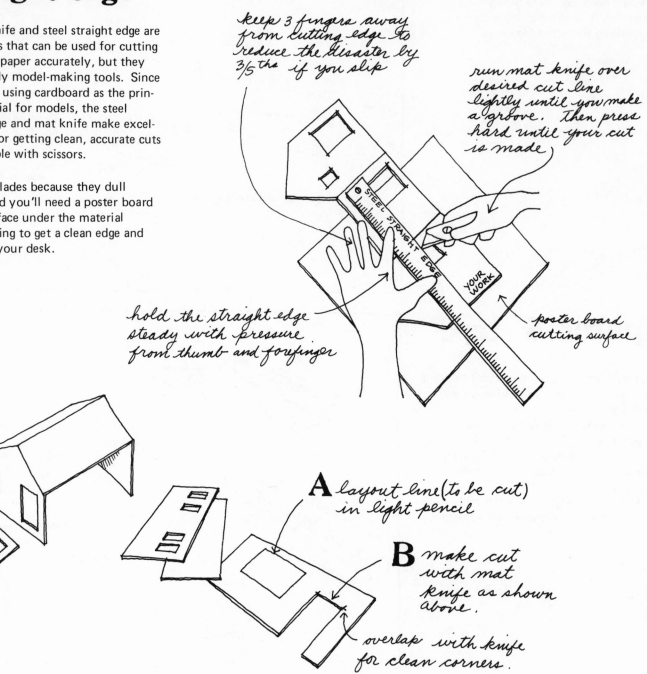

keep 3 fingers away from cutting edge to reduce the disaster by 3/5 ths if you slip

run mat knife over desired cut line lightly until you make a groove. Then press hard until your cut is made

STEEL STRAIGHT EDGE

YOUR WORK

poster board cutting surface

hold the straight edge steady with pressure from thumb and forefinger

A layout line (to be cut) in light pencil

B make cut with mat knife as shown above.

overlap with knife for clean corners.

scales

Architects use a scale, or ruler, as a tool to reduce objects (buildings) to a size that will fit on a drawing. A one-quarter inch line on the drawing might represent one foot of the actual building.

In other words, if you choose the one-quarter inch equals one foot reduction scale on the ruler, a twelve foot wall would be drawn as twelve-quarters of an inch, and appear on your drawing as three inches long.

There are eleven different scales on the ruler that you can experiment with to arrive at one that will make it possible to fit all you want to draw on the page.

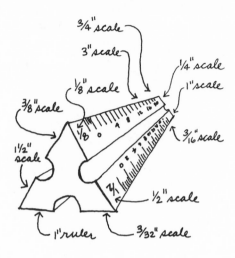

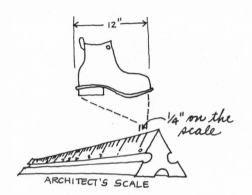

ARCHITECT'S SCALE

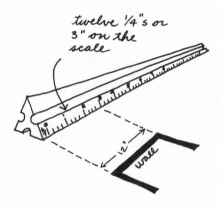

twelve ¼"s or 3" on the scale

Four feet would be equal to four-quarters of one inch, or one inch on the drawing.

If you decide that the three inch line is too small and hard to work with, you might choose a scale of one-half inch equals one foot. This would reduce the twelve foot wall twenty-four times to a six inch line on the drawing.

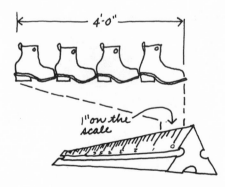

1" on the scale

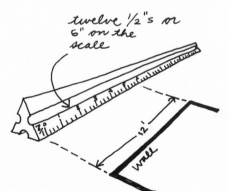

twelve ½"s or 6" on the scale

DRAWING

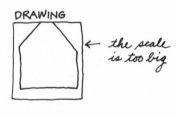

the scale is too big

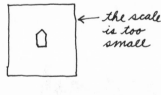

the scale is too small

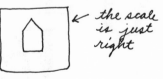

the scale is just right

23

sign marker

The sign marker is one of those tools that you really don't need but you'll enjoy working with. It is a rubber stamp alphabet of letters, numbers, and punctuation marks, each with its own wooden handle.

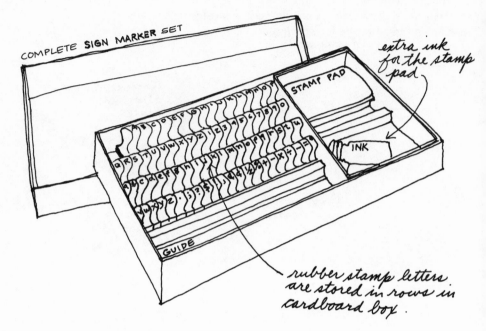

COMPLETE SIGN MARKER SET

STAMP PAD

INK

GUIDE

extra ink for the stamp pad

rubber stamp letters are stored in rows in cardboard box.

They are fun to use for making titles and writing letters to your friends.

We used three sign markers to make all the titles in this book. One-quarter inch for the small lettering, three-eighth inch for the medium, and one-half inch for the large.

Dear Peter,

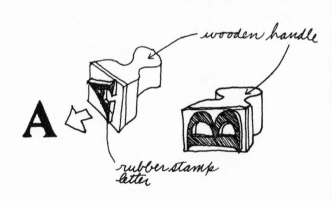

wooden handle

A

rubber stamp letter

For source of sign markers, see appendix.

2. Gathering Information

It will help in your design if you develop a visual sense. Some people tend to be more knowledgeable in this area than others. But even if you feel inadequate there are ways to develop your visual sense. In this chapter we are going to show you how.

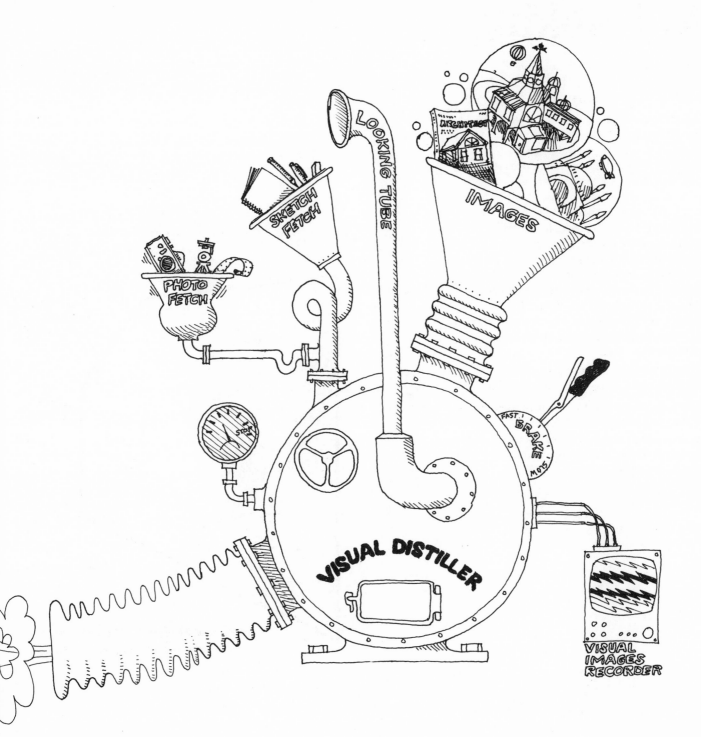

A. Looking

How you see and what you observe is very important. You can teach yourself to be more visually observant.

Look at inside and outside spaces you like. Ask yourself why you like them. Study what is going on in the space. How does the light enter? What does it bounce off? How are color and texture used? What is the feeling—open? intimate? Try asking yourself these questions as you look. Travel to historical architectural landmarks (you can find architectural guide books for most major cities) and spend time just looking. One way to develop your visual comprehension is to look at a building for a while; then without looking, try to draw it. Then compare what you've drawn to the building.

Look through architectural magazines. These provide excellent sources for ideas.

See the appendix for the names of some architectural magazines. Newsstand magazines that feature houses are also good to examine. Clip things you like for future reference.

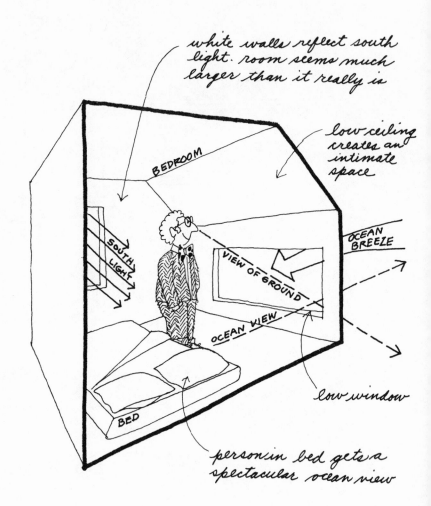

white walls reflect south light. room seems much larger than it really is

low ceiling creates an intimate space

BEDROOM

SOUTH LIGHT

VIEW OF GROUND

OCEAN BREEZE

OCEAN VIEW

low window

BED

person in bed gets a spectacular ocean view

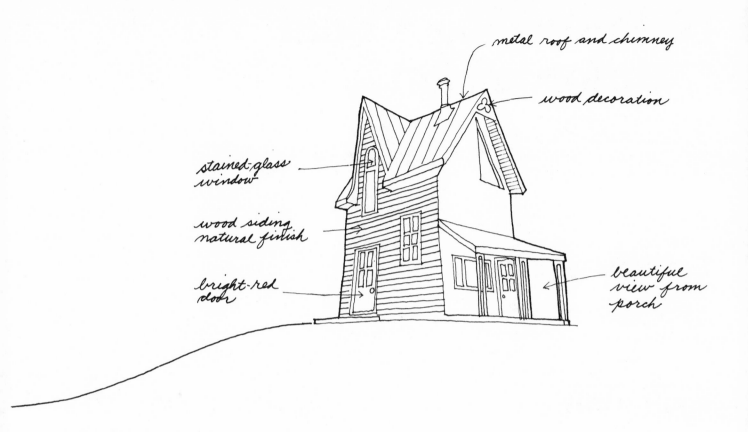

metal roof and chimney

wood decoration

stained-glass window

wood siding natural finish

bright-red door

beautiful view from porch

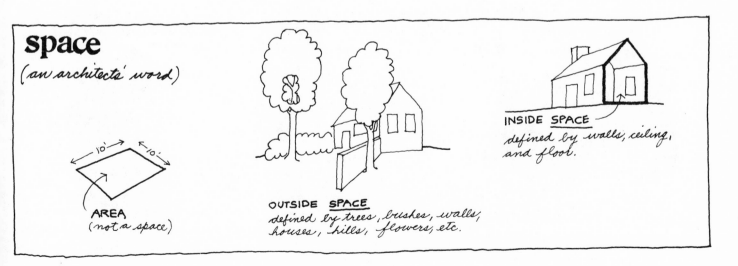

space

(an architects' word)

AREA
(not a space)

OUTSIDE SPACE
defined by trees, brushes, walls, houses, hills, flowers, etc.

INSIDE SPACE
defined by walls, ceiling, and floor.

B. Recording Visual Information

There are basically two ways to record what you see. Photography and drawing. Both are very important art forms that will develop your visual abilities.

1. Photography

As you travel, photograph places you like. They provide a record for future reference.

equipment

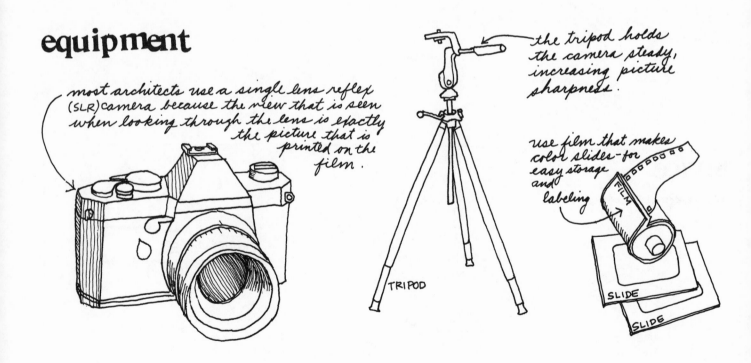

most architects use a single lens reflex (SLR) camera because the view that is seen when looking through the lens is exactly the picture that is printed on the film.

the tripod holds the camera steady, increasing picture sharpness.

use film that makes color slides—for easy storage and labeling

TRIPOD

FILM

SLIDE

SLIDE

Panoramic view

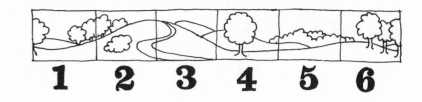

1 2 3 4 5 6

Photography is also useful in recording your building site. By setting the camera on a tripod and rotating it after each picture, a panoramic view can be pasted together to reveal the whole site.

to make a panoramic photograph, the camera is set on the tripod and rotated after each picture is taken so that the second picture begins where the first one ended. and so on.

the prints are then pasted or taped together to make a 360° continuous view.

ROTATE CAMERA

1
2
3

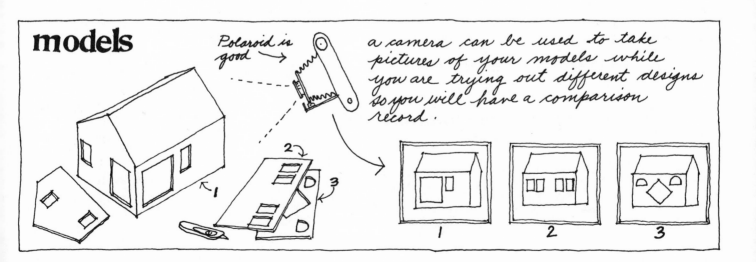

models

Polaroid is good →

Polaroid is good →

a camera can be used to take pictures of your models while you are trying out different designs so you will have a comparison record.

1   2   3

2. Drawing

Drawing is one of the most important skills to develop because it is the simplest form of visual communication. The best way to develop it is to do it. Drawing buildings from life is an excellent exercise. It is not too important what materials you use - soft drawing pencils or felt tip pens, even a ball point. Find something you're comfortable working with. Any paper will do.

Take the time to look carefully at what you are drawing. How is each element related to the others? Note that there are basic shape outlines, textures, shades, and shadows.

Perspective drawing is an attempt to represent a three-dimensional object on a two-dimension piece of paper.

You need not always do complete drawings. Often a small detail sketch, perhaps with a note, will record just what you want to remember.

For more detailed information, see *Architectural Graphic Standards*. (See appendix.)

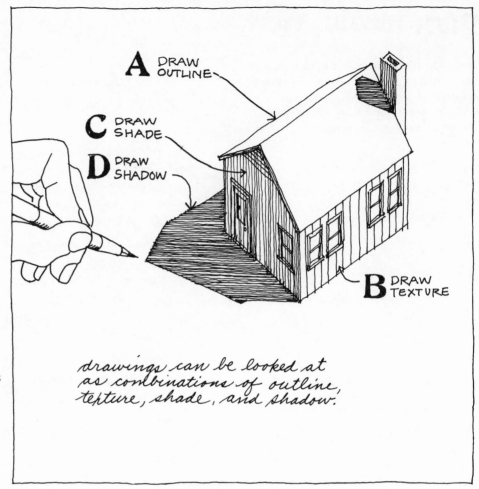

A DRAW OUTLINE

C DRAW SHADE

D DRAW SHADOW

B DRAW TEXTURE

drawings can be looked at as combinations of outline, texture, shade, and shadow.

tools

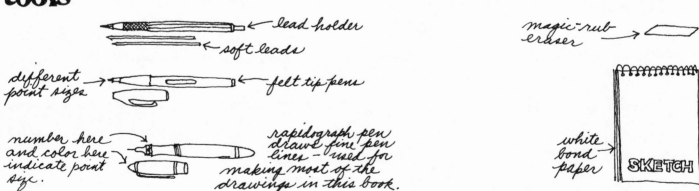

lead holder

soft leads

different point sizes

felt tip pens

number here and color here indicate point size.

rapidograph pen draws fine pen lines - used for making most of the drawings in this book.

magic-rub eraser

white bond paper

SKETCH

four ways to record a room

When you are in a room that you really like you can record it using one of the methods listed below.

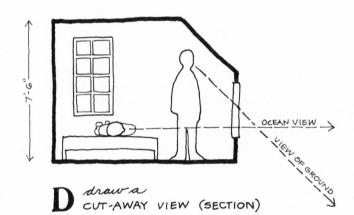

A *draw a*
TOP VIEW (PLAN)

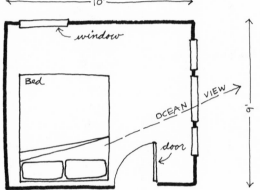

B *draw a*
SEE-THRU LINE SKETCH

D *draw a*
CUT-AWAY VIEW (SECTION)

C *draw views of the*
4 WALLS (ELEVATIONS)

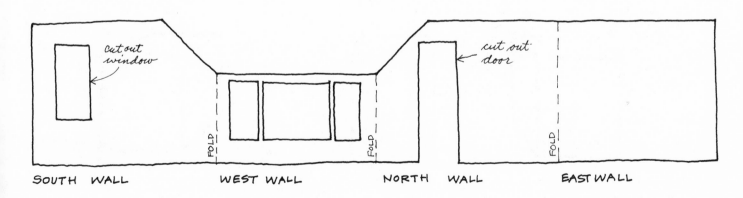

SOUTH WALL   WEST WALL   NORTH WALL   EAST WALL

one-point perspective drawing

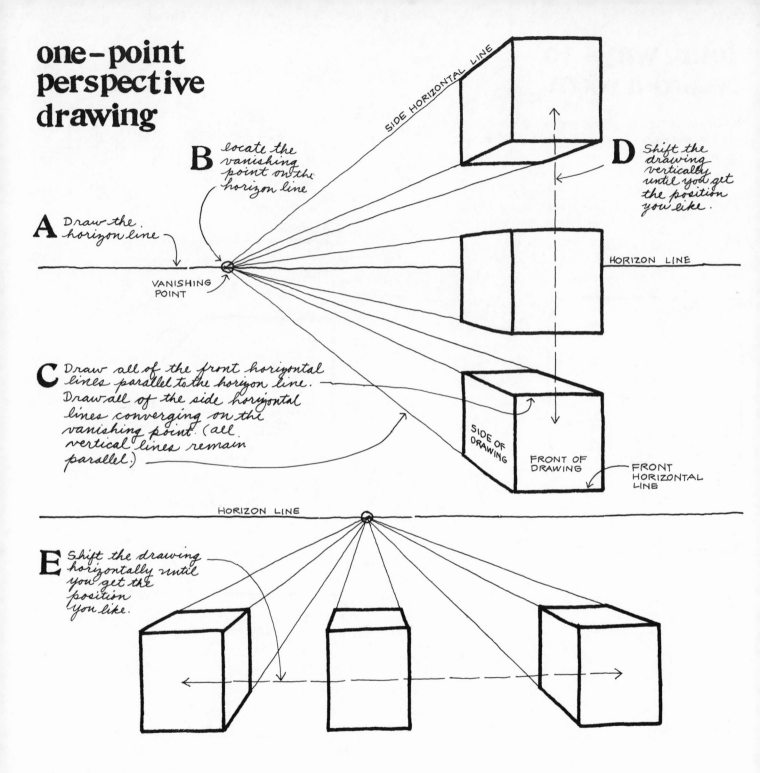

A Draw the horizon line

VANISHING POINT

B locate the vanishing point on the horizon line

SIDE HORIZONTAL LINE

D Shift the drawing vertically until you get the position you like.

HORIZON LINE

C Draw all of the front horizontal lines parallel to the horizon line. Draw all of the side horizontal lines converging on the vanishing point. (all vertical lines remain parallel.)

SIDE OF DRAWING

FRONT OF DRAWING

FRONT HORIZONTAL LINE

HORIZON LINE

E Shift the drawing horizontally until you get the position you like.

two-point perspective drawing

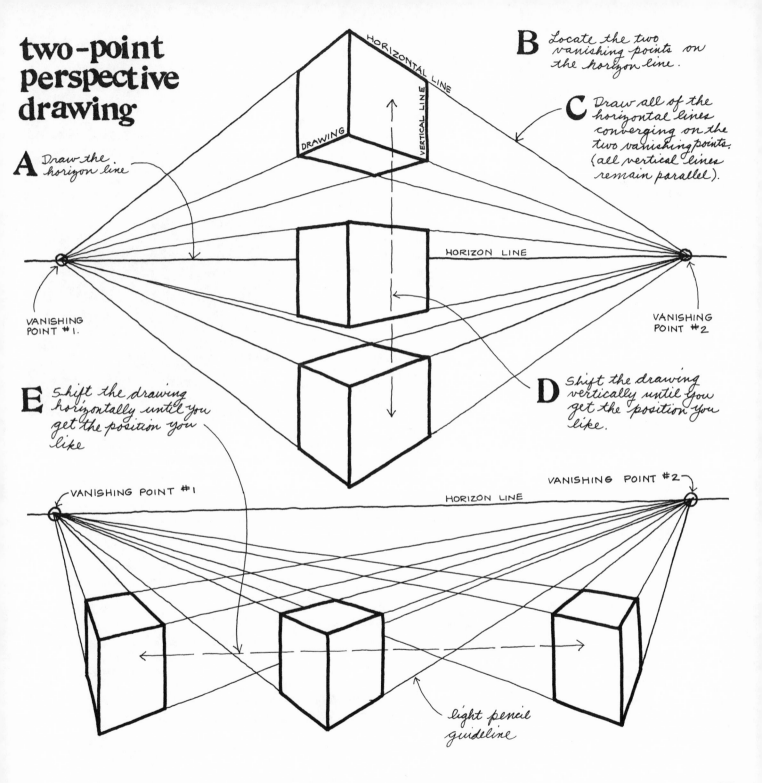

A Draw the horizon line

B Locate the two vanishing points on the horizon line.

C Draw all of the horizontal lines converging on the two vanishing points. (all vertical lines remain parallel).

D Shift the drawing vertically until you get the position you like.

E Shift the drawing horizontally until you get the position you like

HORIZONTAL LINE

VERTICAL LINE

DRAWING

HORIZON LINE

VANISHING POINT #1.

VANISHING POINT #2

VANISHING POINT #1

VANISHING POINT #2

HORIZON LINE

light pencil guideline

C. Keeping a Notebook

Start a notebook for things like magazine clippings, photographs, and sketches. It can be one of the already bound drawing books sold at art supply stores or a loose leaf notebook.

Put in things that you *like*.

The notebook will serve as reference later on when you are designing.

don't like painted wood on outside of house. would rather have natural weathered wood

AESTHETIC of farmhouses with big porches

like vines growing over house and lots of plants and flowers

don't like shutters unless they're necessary

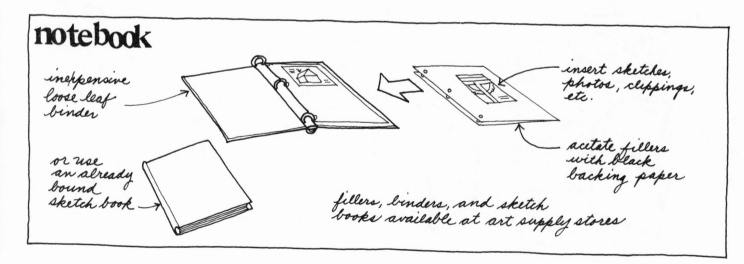

notebook

inexpensive loose leaf binder

or use an already bound sketch book

insert sketches, photos, clippings, etc.

acetate fillers with black backing paper

fillers, binders, and sketch books available at art supply stores

D. Dreams

Up to this point we have been discussing visual information that comes from outside. Another rich source of information that you already have are your dreams. The subconscious, especially, is a rich source of visual images. Let your mind wander and your most fantastic ideas come out.

3. Designing

Designing is a process that involves the collecting of information, the evaluation of information, and decision making based on that evaluation. You will be constantly re-evaluating your design as new ideas occur.

In this chapter we will demonstrate how to design by giving you the principles, such as how to analyze and draw the site, how to list your needs, how to work with blobs of space (bubbles) to develop ideas. We will describe and illustrate how to use models and drawings to represent your design.

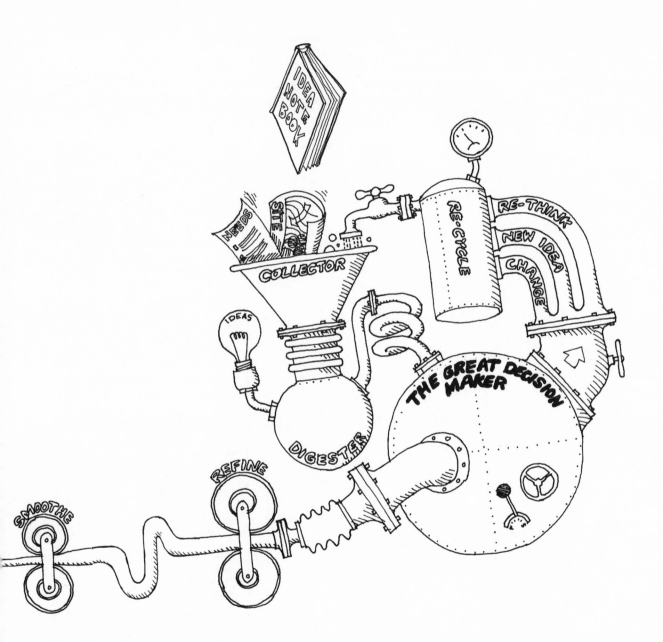

A. Site Drawing

Spend a day at your site with a soft pencil and yellow tracing paper, sketching the location of property lines, ground slope, roads, utility locations, existing buildings (including neighbors), trees, ponds, streams, and other natural features.

Site conditions play an important role in influencing the shape of your house. You should make a diligent attempt to record as many as possible. The more you draw, the more you discover, the better your design, the richer the final result - in that order.

Here are a few ways to draw the conditions listed above.

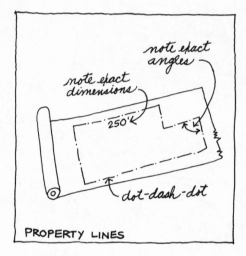

PROPERTY LINES

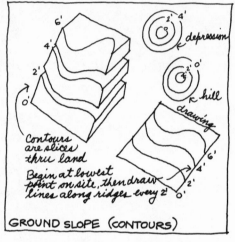

GROUND SLOPE (CONTOURS)

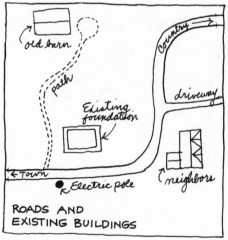

ROADS AND EXISTING BUILDINGS

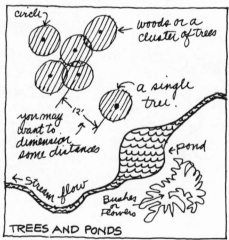

TREES AND PONDS

Next, you must determine the sun's movement, view directions, and summer breezes and winter storm directions. You may also want to indicate directions of undesirable noise or pollution. If it is impossible to gather this information by camping on your land, talk to neighbors or others who might be familiar with your site conditions.

Here's how to draw them:

You may want to take this sketch information and make a neat, accurate drawing with felt tip pens on the good-quality tracing paper. Use your T-square and triangle to lay out the property lines correctly. Use your architect's scale to reduce dimensions accurately.

Site drawings are done to a small scale; usually one-sixteenth inch equals one foot, zero inches.

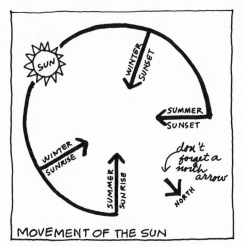

MOVEMENT OF THE SUN

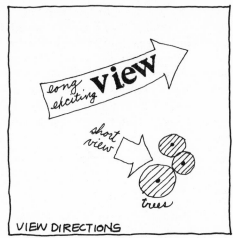

VIEW DIRECTIONS

SUMMER BREEZES AND WINTER STORMS

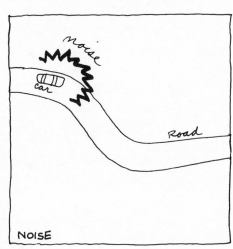

NOISE

site model
make at ⅟₁₆"=1'-0" scale

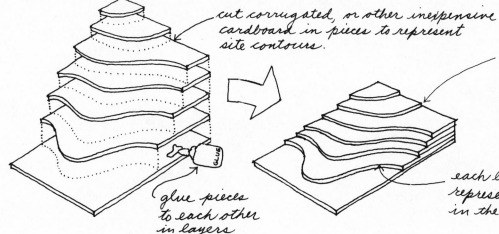

cut corrugated, or other inexpensive cardboard in pieces to represent site contours.

glue pieces to each other in layers

measure the thickness of the cardboard using the scale of the model. using the ⅟₁₆"=1'-0" scale, ⅛" thick cardboard would be a rise of 2'.

each layer of cardboard represents a rise in the land.

Now begins the story of Fred and Lois and their family. They have just bought three acres of beautiful country property. It has a spring-fed pond, rolling hills in an already cleared meadow, and woods of deciduous and evergreen trees. There is a nice view of distant mountains, and this is where they intend to build their dream house.

Here is a photograph of their land.

Fred and Lois camp out on their site to fully experience their land. They observe how the sun moves, and where the noises come from. They walk around experiencing the different views. They decide they want to build near the pond for aesthetic and recreational reasons.

Fred and Lois make their site drawing analysis at the site, then at home, felt tip pen drawing shown here.

Now they were ready to write their program.

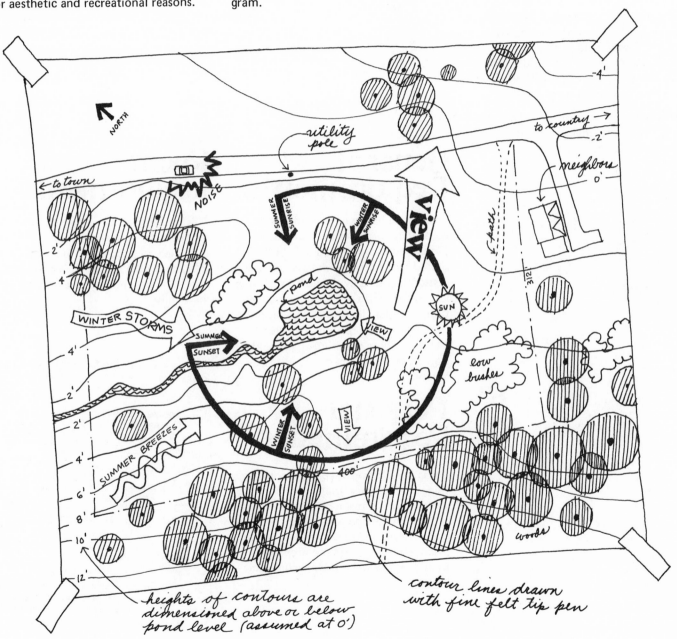

NORTH

utility pole

to country →

← to town

NOISE

neighbors

SUMMER SUNRISE

WINTER SUNRISE

VIEW

pond

SUN

path

312

WINTER STORMS

SUMMER SUNSET

VIEW

low bushes

4'

2'

4'

2'

2'

4'

SUMMER BREEZES

WINTER SUNSET

VIEW

6'

8'

400

10'

12'

woods

heights of contours are dimensioned above or below pond level (assumed at 0')

contour lines drawn with fine felt tip pen

-4'

-2'

0'

-2'

B. Program
Listing Your Needs

A program is a *written* description of what you think your design should be like. It should include all your ideas about outside places and inside rooms from the general (such as aesthetics) to the specific (such as room size).

There are three ways of breaking down the requirements that you must list in order to have a complete program:

General Requirements

These are a listing of ideas about the home in general (for example, how it should look from the outside or how it should feel on the inside) and some suggestions about how the home should relate to the group of people living there. (For example, does it need an outdoor living place and are all meals eaten together?) These requirements should be worked out by *all* members of the family.

Personal Requirements

These are a listing of spaces, rooms, or things in the house that a particular person requires to make his/her living easier. (For example, one person may be an avid piano player and might require a quiet place to play.) These requirements should be worked out by each person himself.

Room Requirements

This is a simple chart of all the predicted rooms in the house with as many descriptive categories necessary to explain everything about the room. This chart too should be worked out by *all* members of the family.

Here is an idea of what this room chart looks like:

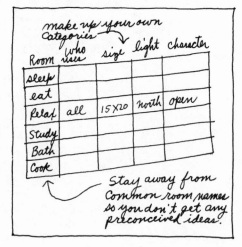

make up your own Categories

Room	who uses	size	light	character
sleep				
eat				
Relax	all	15 X 20	north	open
Study				
Bath				
Cook				

Stay away from common room names so you don't get any preconceived ideas.

The Sample family sits down together
one evening and talks about what everybody wants from the house. They write
the program shown on this page and the
next.

General Requirements

New England _Salt Box house_. the look of the But we do want some very large glass areas. We want _natural light_ in every room. Every room should feel "light and airy". We all like skylights and lots of plants. natural wood finish on inside and outside of house as much as possible.

$35,000 budget

We like high spaces inside and a big living room for parties. We want a beautiful- functional _kitchen_. It is important to us to have a place to have _meals together_.

We must have a good place to have summer fun- outside- observable from the kitchen because of kids.

PICNICS

necessary to have a place for laundry area. Also covered entry porch for bad weather. Extra storage in every room.

Now Fred and Lois are ready to begin playing with bubble diagrams.

C. Bubble Diagrams

Using an Architectural Technique to Study Room Arrangements

The next step, after doing the program chart, is to begin working with bubble diagrams.

The method is to represent spaces with amorphous blob-like shapes. This is because you are only *exploring* the relationships between spaces at this point. A more distinct shape will come later.

Draw bubbles from the spaces in the room chart and arrange them in various ways to explore different possibilities. You may want to give each function a color to further distinguish the rooms in your diagram. For example, eating could be yellow, sleeping could be blue, and so on.

Another idea is to cut out paper discs and move them around.

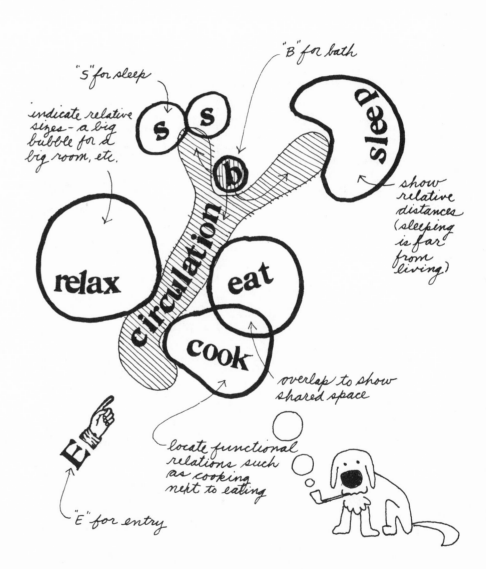

Here are some possible bubble arrangements.

1

Rooms opening off a corridor.
This is a traditional way of organizing space. The drawback is that it wastes space since the corridor cannot be used for anything else.

2

Rooms at opposite ends of a corridor.
This plan is used to achieve a separation, perhaps between quiet and noisy areas.

3

Rooms opening off a large communal room.
This arrangement offers less privacy than some of the others. But it is a more efficient use of space since there are no corridors.

4

Rooms used to enclose a space.
Good for visual privacy or to block winds, or gather breezes.

5

Rooms within a room.
For example, a kitchen and bathroom core, perhaps with a sleeping platform above. This can be an exciting way to develop a large high space.

6

Rooms stacked vertically (such as two- and three-story houses).
Think about where the stairs will be. Consider upper spaces that open to rooms below.

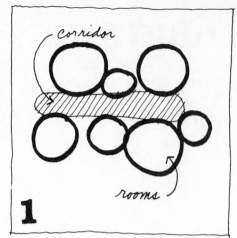

corridor

rooms

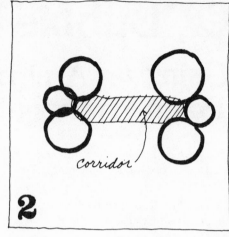

corridor

Big Room

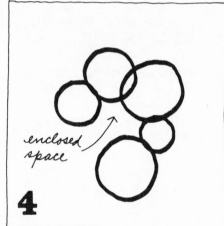

enclosed space

Big room

little rooms inside the big room.

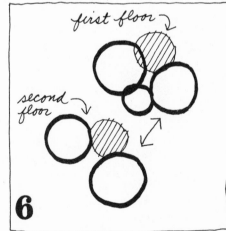

first floor

second floor

3D Bubbles

Still another technique is to cut out paper strips and make bubbles (or other shapes) as shown below. This allows you to explore two or more floor levels.

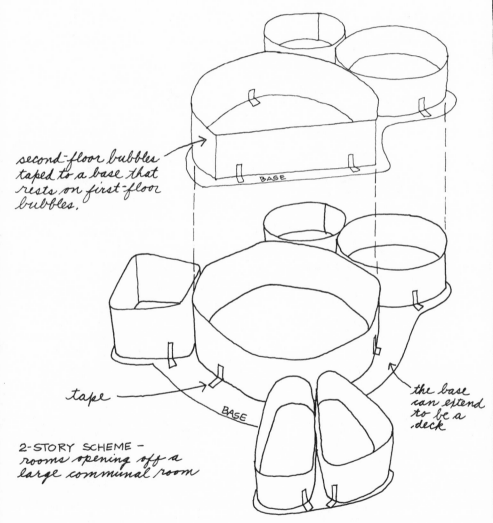

second-floor bubbles taped to a base that rests on first-floor bubbles.

BASE

tape

BASE

the base can extend to be a deck

2-STORY SCHEME — rooms opening off a large communal room

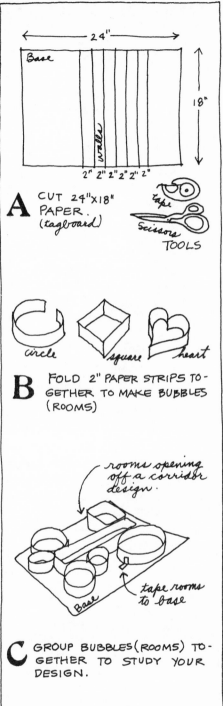

A CUT 24"X18" PAPER. (tagboard)

tape

scissors

TOOLS

circle *square* *heart*

B FOLD 2" PAPER STRIPS TO- GETHER TO MAKE BUBBLES (ROOMS)

rooms opening off a corridor design.

tape rooms to base

Base

C GROUP BUBBLES (ROOMS) TO- GETHER TO STUDY YOUR DESIGN.

Site Planning Principles

Once you feel comfortable sketching room relationships this way, begin to work with bubbles on your site. Here are some site planning principles that will help in laying out your bubbles.

These are very general principles and there will be times when you will want to do just the opposite.

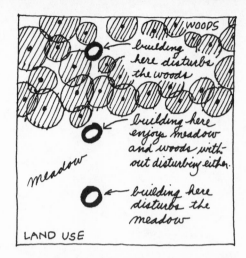

WOODS

building here disturbs the woods

building here enjoys meadow and woods without disturbing either.

meadow

building here disturbs the meadow

LAND USE

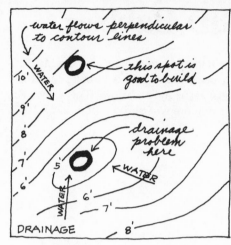

water flows perpendicular to contour lines

this spot is good to build

drainage problem here

WATER

DRAINAGE

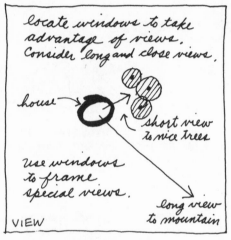

locate windows to take advantage of views. Consider long and close views.

house

short view to nice trees

use windows to frame special views.

long view to mountain

VIEW

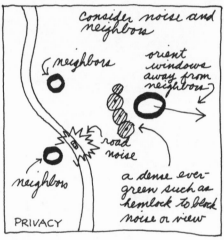

consider noise and neighbors

neighbors

orient windows away from neighbors

road noise

neighbors

a dense evergreen such as hemlock to block noise or view

PRIVACY

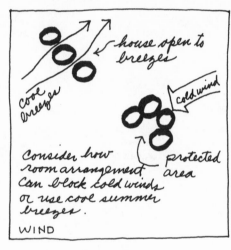

house open to breezes

cool breezes

cold wind

Consider how room arrangement can block cold winds or use cool summer breezes.

protected area

WIND

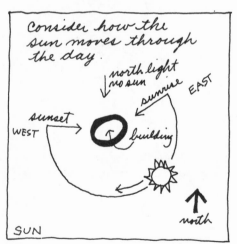

Consider how the sun moves through the day.

north light no sun

sunrise

EAST

sunset

WEST

building

north

SUN

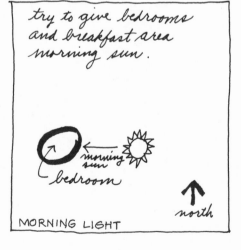

try to give bedrooms and breakfast area morning sun.

morning sun

bedroom

north

MORNING LIGHT

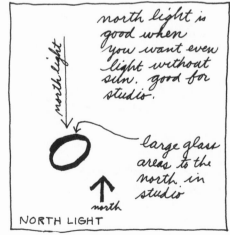

north light is good when you want even light without sun. good for studio.

north light

large glass areas to the north in studio

north

NORTH LIGHT

Now that you have the site plan drawn, your program written, and you understand bubble diagrams, combine all that information by drawing bubble diagrams over your site drawing, using yellow tracing paper. This way the bubbles can relate to elements on the land. We'll use Fred and Lois's site to show you what we mean.

Fred and Lois decide that they want the house near the pond. They draw this area on a larger scale and try the following bubble or room arrangements.

The first spot was chosen because it has a south orientation to the pond, allowing a view of the pond and sun all day.

The bubbles indicate a room arrangement showing *rooms opening off a corridor*, arranged so that the children's bedrooms get early morning light and the master bedroom gets north light. The kitchen, dining, and living area get south light and a view of the pond. The orientation gives a minimal face to the cold winds. The living room gets the long view to the west. The negative aspects of this plan are that the house is too close to road noise and pollution and is not secluded enough.

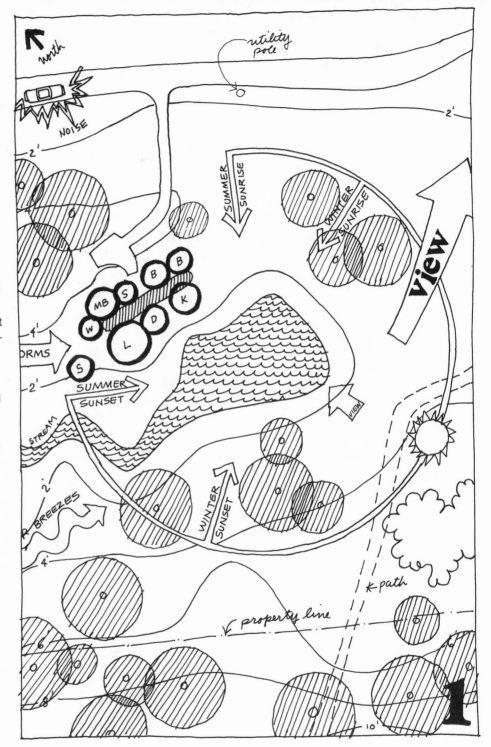

The second spot was chosen because it
takes advantage of the pond. It also has
three beautiful oak trees. The bubble
diagram shows *rooms at opposite ends of
a corridor.* This gives a separation between the public noisy areas of kitchen,
living and dining, and the quiet bedroom and studio/study areas. The living
and dining rooms are located to get mid-
day and afternoon sun and views of the
pond. The long plan makes maximum
use of summer breezes. The negative
aspect is that it will be more costly to
build and heat since the design sprawls.

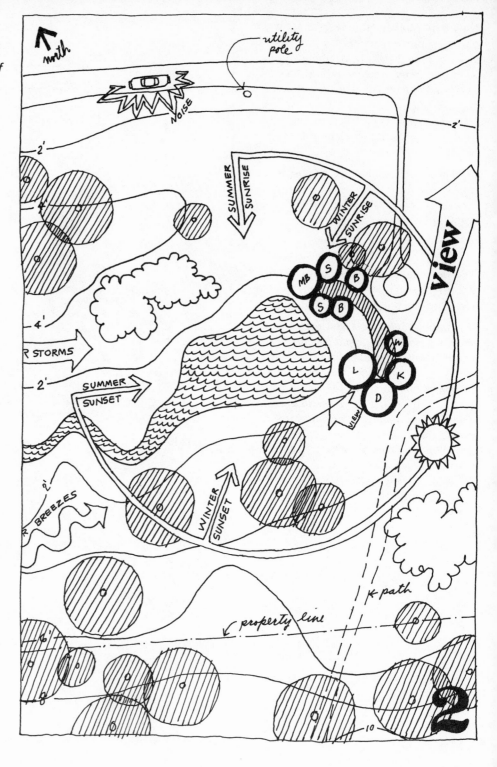

Fred and Lois work until they feel they have considered most possibilities.

Then they analyze their drawings and choose the one that appears to have the potential to fulfill most of their requirements.

Shown here, the bubble diagram indicates a house that is away from the road and tucked back against the woods for privacy. It has good views in all directions and uses the pond without disturbing it.

The bubble arrangement shows a combination of rooms within a room, rooms around a common room, and vertical separation of the floors. The second floor maximizes the long view and provides maximum natural light in the bedrooms.

The living room has an intimate view of the woods to the west and long exciting views to the northeast.

The location also makes use of the existing path.

Now they are ready to turn their bubble diagram into a design.

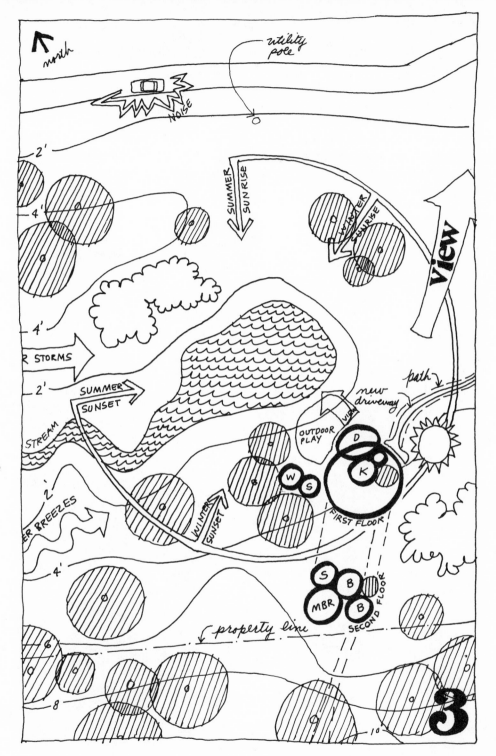

D. Design Principles

The following pages in this chapter will demonstrate how to turn your program and bubble diagram into a design.

But first there are some basic principles to consider that concern sun, ventilation, light, and space.

1. Ventilation

The fact that air expands as it heats up causes it to become lighter and to rise. This effect, known as the stack effect, is very useful in designing for natural ventilation.

By providing a higher outlet in the house for warmer air, you draw in cooler air through outlets down below. The cool air fills the void left by the rising warm air.

Another point to remember is that cross ventilation works best at an angle closer to 45º to the wind rather than normal (90º) to it since more air is drawn out of the downwind side by low pressure, causing air to be drawn in the upwind side. The biggest windows should actually be on the downwind side.

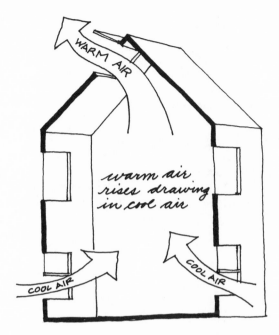

warm air rises drawing in cool air

WARM AIR

COOL AIR

COOL AIR

THE STACK EFFECT

BREEZE

a casement window can be used to grab a breeze

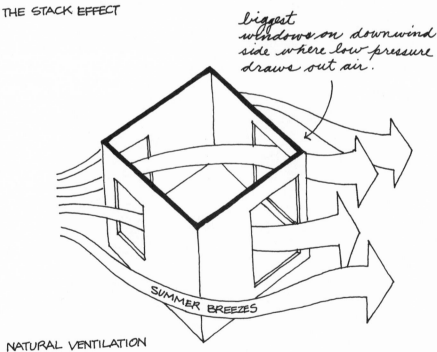

biggest windows on downwind side where low pressure draws out air.

SUMMER BREEZES

NATURAL VENTILATION

2. Climate

For hot climates - insulate the west, the south, and the roof. Provide good ventilation. Block natural sun coming through the windows outside the house. Use light colors, since these reflect the sun. An overhanging roof is a good way to control the sun in hot climates.

For cold climates - insulate everywhere. Use double or triple pane glass on all windows. At night plan for curtains on windows to prevent radiation heat loss. Use dark colors; they absorb the sun and re-radiate the heat.

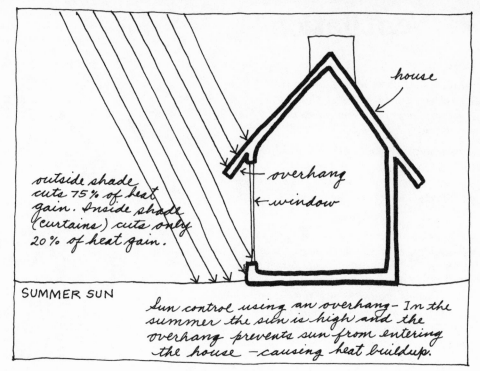

house

overhang

window

outside shade cuts 75% of heat gain. Inside shade (curtains) cuts only 20% of heat gain.

SUMMER SUN

Sun control using an overhang— In the summer the sun is high and the overhang prevents sun from entering the house —causing heat buildup.

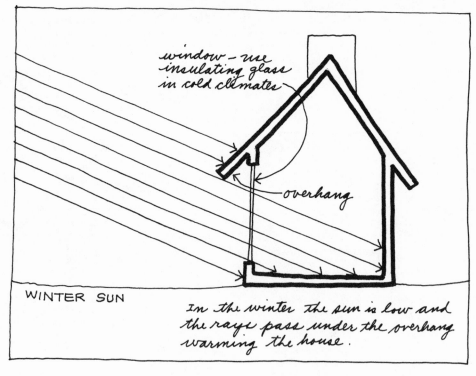

window — use insulating glass in cold climates

overhang

WINTER SUN

In the winter the sun is low and the rays pass under the overhang warming the house.

Deciduous trees are good for sun control since they form a shade in the summer and then lose their leaves in the winter allowing sun to warm the house.

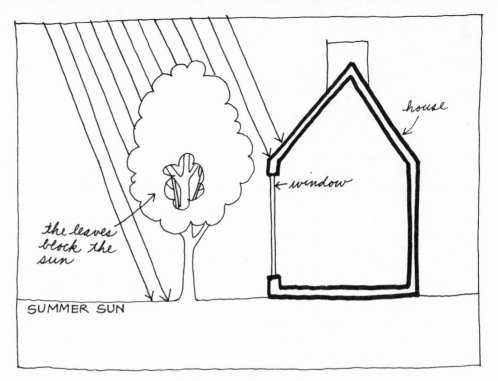

the leaves block the sun

house

window

SUMMER SUN

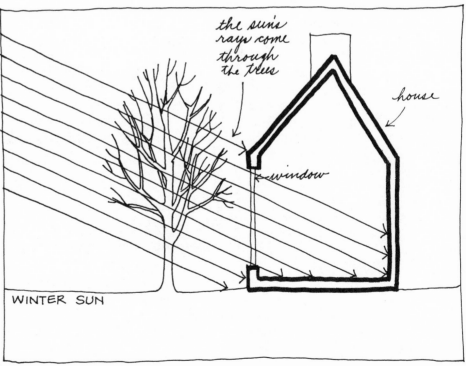

the sun's rays come through the trees

house

window

WINTER SUN

3. Space

A house can be made to include many different spaces, some light, some dark, high, low, rough, smooth, etc. Many spaces are purely personal, some functional, some poetic.

There are certain psychological responses to space which you can discover if you look around. A dark, low, or cave-like space gives a protected, introverted feeling, perhaps stemming from caveman days. The opposite is a light, high, open space, an extroverted space. These are simplified extremes. There are many other possibilities, but a house that provides more of the *different* kinds of space experience will be more interesting.

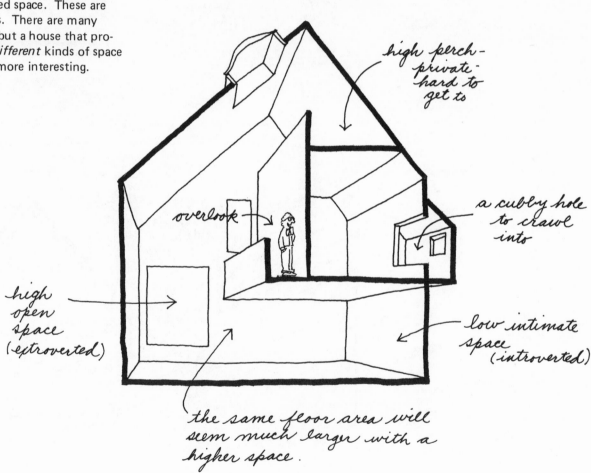

high perch - private - hard to get to

overlook

a cubby hole to crawl into

high open space (extroverted)

low intimate space (introverted)

the same floor area will seem much larger with a higher space.

4. Movement

A house is not something static to be looked at, but rather something that you move through. Think of it as choreography of space, changing vistas moving from high to low, dark to light, etc.

When you stand near a window and look out, there's a wide view, but when you are across the room sitting at a table, you see a narrow particular view through the same window. Passing from a high to a low space you are most aware of the difference at the moment you cross between, and each emphasizes the other. Think about how you will move through the spaces and the changing vistas.

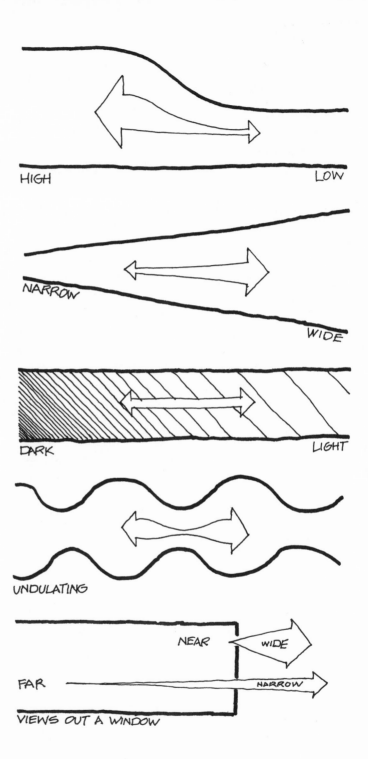

HIGH   LOW

NARROW   WIDE

DARK   LIGHT

UNDULATING

NEAR   WIDE

FAR   NARROW

VIEWS OUT A WINDOW

5. Shape

The overall shape of your house will be a result of many different forces: what goes on inside, the climate, the site, the materials used, and what visual images you want to create.

At right are some of the traditional basic shapes.

Other possibilities include hemisphere, cylinders, polygons, etc.

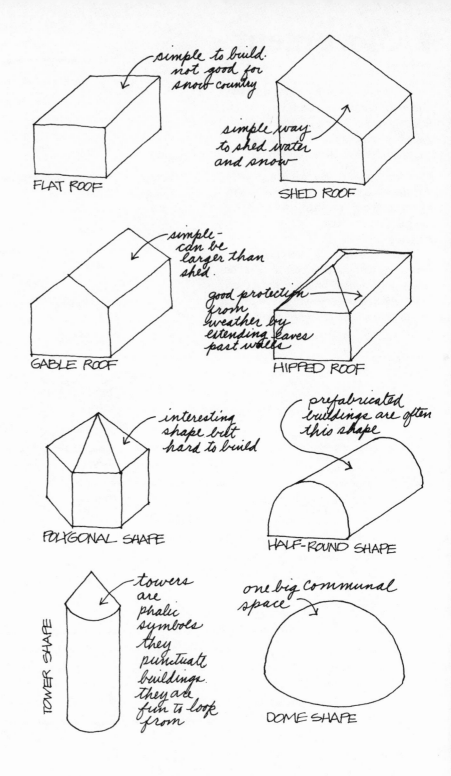

simple to build. not good for snow country

FLAT ROOF

simple way to shed water and snow

SHED ROOF

simple — can be larger than shed.

GABLE ROOF

good protection from weather by extending eaves past walls

HIPPED ROOF

interesting shape but hard to build

POLYGONAL SHAPE

prefabricated buildings are often this shape

HALF-ROUND SHAPE

towers are phalic symbols they punctuate buildings. they are fun to look from

TOWER SHAPE

one big communal space

DOME SHAPE

6. Combined Shapes

Complex shapes can usually be thought of as combinations of the more simple shapes shown on the preceding page. Here are some examples.

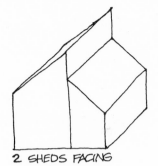

2 SHEDS FACING

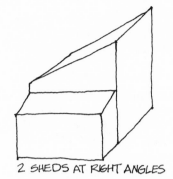

2 SHEDS AT RIGHT ANGLES

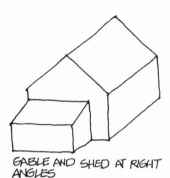

GABLE AND SHED AT RIGHT ANGLES

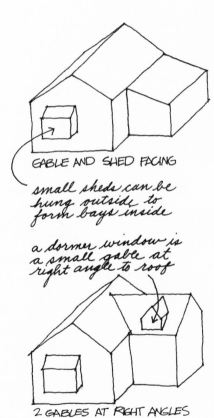

GABLE AND SHED FACING

small sheds can be hung outside to form bays inside

a dormer window is a small gable at right angle to roof

2 GABLES AT RIGHT ANGLES

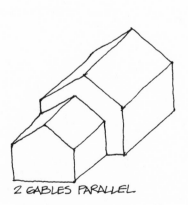

2 GABLES PARALLEL

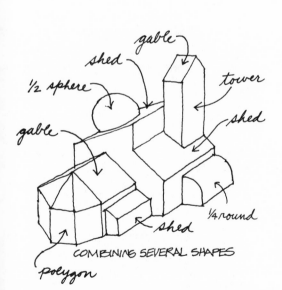

gable

shed

½ sphere

tower

gable

shed

shed

¼ round

COMBINING SEVERAL SHAPES

polygon

7. Light

People think of light as something that comes in a window. When they want more light, they put in a bigger window. But there are many ways light can enter a space, and change the space. A high window creates a different light effect than a low window. A deep window, or bay window, will be different from a shallow window. The color of the walls, floor, and ceiling is very important since much room light is actually reflected light.

The lighter the color the more light you get in the room - this is especially important where artificial lighting is used. People often don't realize how much more energy it takes to light a darkly painted room.

Skylighting or angled lighting create different and often dramatic effects. There are many ways to bring in light from above, such as light wells, which act as funneling tubes.

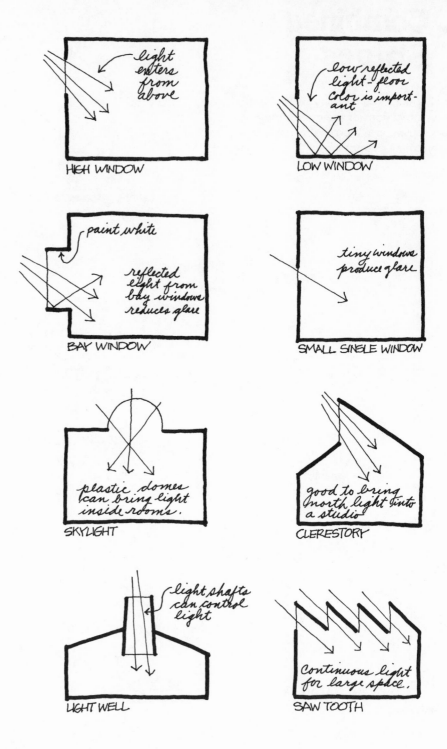

HIGH WINDOW — *light enters from above*

LOW WINDOW — *low reflected light - floor color is important*

BAY WINDOW — *paint white* / *reflected light from bay windows reduces glare*

SMALL SINGLE WINDOW — *tiny windows produce glare*

SKYLIGHT — *plastic domes can bring light inside rooms.*

CLERESTORY — *good to bring north light into a studio*

LIGHT WELL — *light shafts can control light*

SAW TOOTH — *continuous light for large space.*

E. Defining Shape

With the previous principles in mind, you are prepared to tackle the most exciting and important step, the integration of all the information about site, program, function, etc., with your artistic visual images and dreams. It is this synthesis of function and aesthetics that makes architecture a unique art.

Below is an illustration showing the process that begins with bubble diagrams and arrives at a final design.

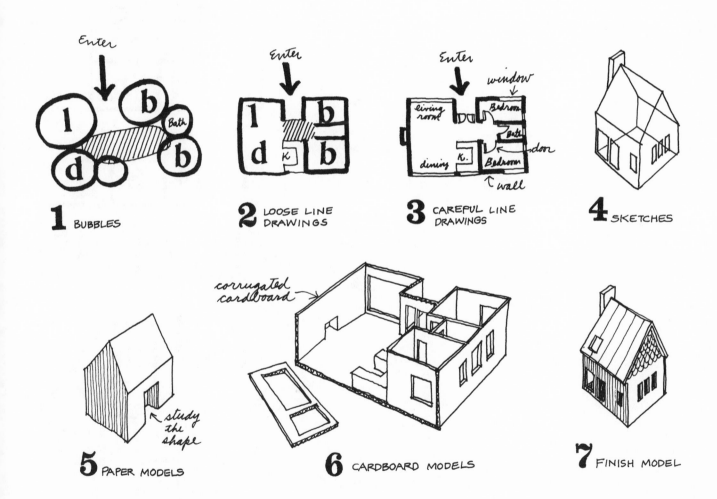

1 BUBBLES

2 LOOSE LINE DRAWINGS

3 CAREFUL LINE DRAWINGS

4 SKETCHES

5 PAPER MODELS

6 CARDBOARD MODELS

7 FINISH MODEL

1. The Plan

Now you are ready to begin to determine
the shape of the plan. Start with the
bubble diagram and see what plan arrangements are suggested. Start with
simple line drawings, drawing freely at
first. Remember that the bubble diagram is only a tool to help you organize
your thoughts. You can change spatial
relationships at any time.

Bubble diagrams suggest relationships.
The actual shapes that can evolve are
limitless. Three different plans from the
same bubble are shown here.

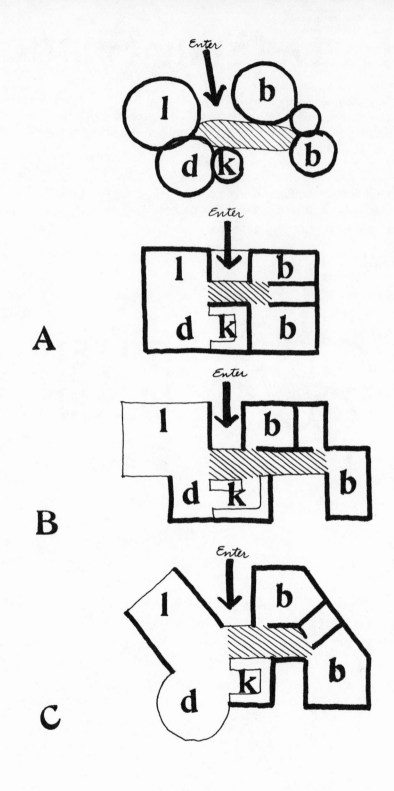

2. Symbols

As your plan evolves, begin to locate doors, windows, bathroom and kitchen fixtures, closets, etc. Here is how to indicate these items on the plan.

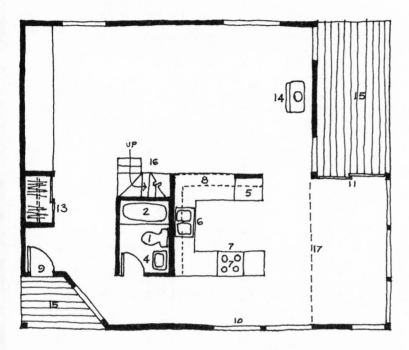

bath

1. TOILET

2. TUB

3. SHOWER

4. SINK

kitchen

5. REFRIGERATOR

6. DOUBLE SINK

7. RANGE

8. SHELVING

house parts

9. DOOR

10. WINDOW

11. SLIDING DOOR

12. FOLDING DOOR

13. CLOSET

14. FRANKLIN STOVE

15. DECK

16. STAIRS
ur

17. WALL ABOVE

18. FIREPLACE

3. Kitchen Planning

On this page are some basic planning principles and dimensions that are important in kitchen planning.

No matter what the shape of the kitchen, there is a basic order that is followed in food preparation. This order must be considered in determining the layout of the sink, refrigerator, range, and counter space.

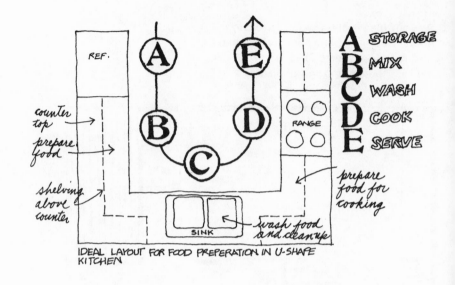

A — STORAGE
B — MIX
C — WASH
D — COOK
E — SERVE

REF.

counter top → prepare food →

shelving above counter →

RANGE

prepare food for cooking

SINK — wash food and clean up

IDEAL LAYOUT FOR FOOD PREPERATION IN U-SHAPE KITCHEN

COUNTER 36"
MIXING 32"
MAX. REACH 72"

VERTICAL HEIGHTS FOR AVERAGE PERSON

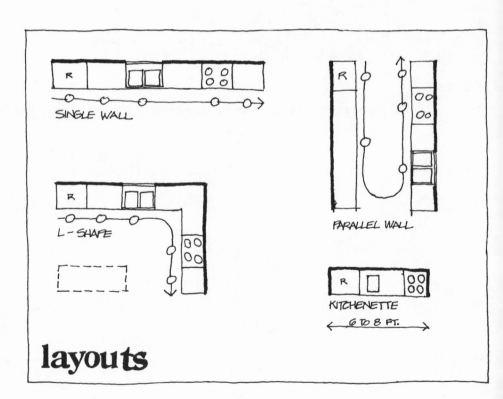

R

SINGLE WALL

R

L-SHAPE

R

PARALLEL WALL

R

KITCHENETTE
6 TO 8 FT.

layouts

4. Bathroom Planning

Here are some basic bathroom planning principles and dimensions. The layouts shown are to give you some examples of common bathroom designs.

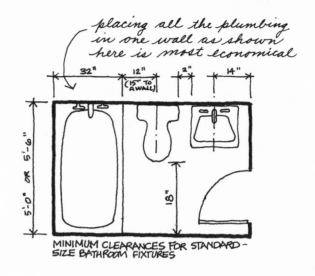

placing all the plumbing in one wall as shown here is most economical

MINIMUM CLEARANCES FOR STANDARD-SIZE BATHROOM FIXTURES

light mirror

VERTICAL DIMENSIONS

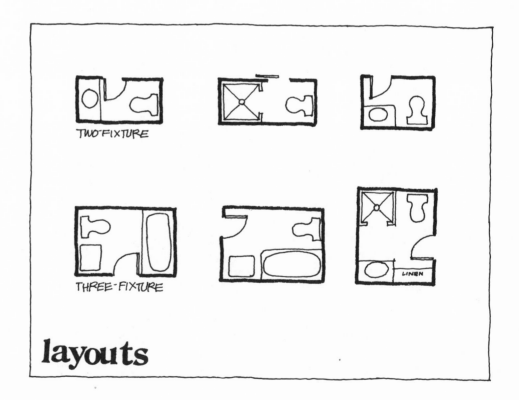

TWO-FIXTURE

THREE-FIXTURE

LINEN

layouts

5. Stairs

Here are some basic principles and dimensions that will help you in designing stairs.

A general rule is that the riser plus the tread should equal 17 to 19 inches. A comfortable stair: 7″ riser, 11″ tread.

The dimensions shown are based on *One and Two Family Dwelling Code*. (See appendix.)

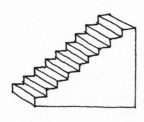

STRAIGHT
easiest to build

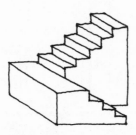

U - SHAPE
used in tight areas

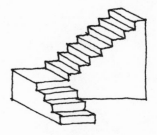

L - SHAPE
used in corners

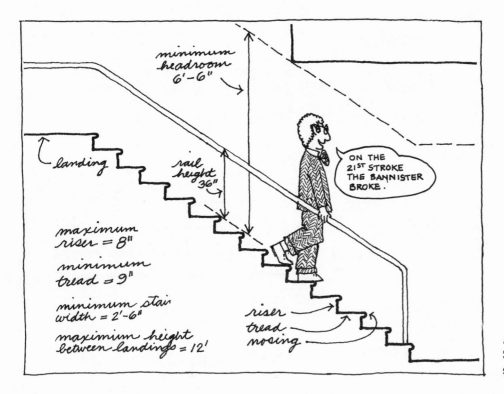

minimum headroom 6′-6″

landing

rail height 36″

ON THE 21ST STROKE THE BANNISTER BROKE.

maximum riser = 8″

minimum tread = 9″

minimum stair width = 2′-6″

maximum height between landings = 12′

riser
tread
nosing

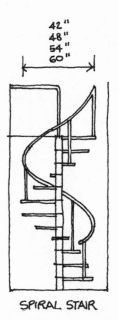

42″
48″
54″
60″

SPIRAL STAIR

A spiral stair can be used for tight spaces. Standard sizes for prefabricated units are shown.

68

6. Furniture Cutouts

As your plan develops, try out furniture arrangements to see how the rooms are working. Here is how to indicate furniture with the sizes given of the more common pieces. Cut out the furniture pieces shown here and move them around on a floor plan drawn to one-quarter inch scale to try different arrangements.

Check to see that there is room for doors and windows to operate properly and that passageways are not obstructed.

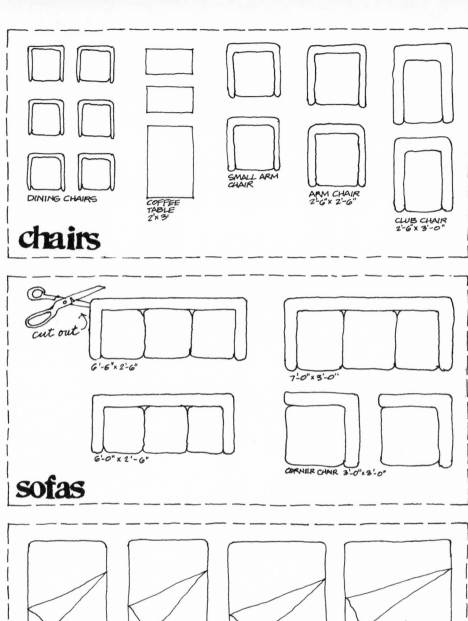

chairs

DINING CHAIRS

COFFEE TABLE 2'x 3'

SMALL ARM CHAIR

ARM CHAIR 2'-6" x 2'-6"

CLUB CHAIR 2'-6 x 3'-0"

sofas

cut out

6'-6" x 2'-6"

7'-0" x 3'-0"

6'-0" x 2'-6"

CORNER CHAIR 3'-0" x 3'-0"

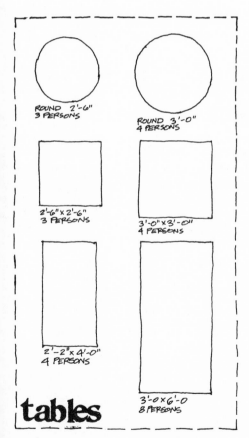

tables

ROUND 2'-6" 3 PERSONS

ROUND 3'-0" 4 PERSONS

2'-6" x 2'-6" 3 PERSONS

3'-0" x 3'-0" 4 PERSONS

2'-2" x 4'-0" 4 PERSONS

3'-0 x 6'-0 8 PERSONS

beds

TWIN 3'-3" x 6'-3"   TWIN

THREE QUARTER 4'-0" x 6'-3"

DOUBLE 4'-6" x 6'-3"

7. Sketches

As you do the plan drawings you should be thinking about what the building's shape will be like.

A way to do this is to draw small, quick sketches, using the plan as a base. These are called *plan oblique drawings* and here is how to make them.

A. The plan is drawn to scale on tracing paper laid over graph paper.

B. The plan is turned on the tracing paper to an angle, such as 30° or 45°. Any angle can be used so that one wall can be more visible than the other.

C. Vertical lines are drawn to scale using the same scale as the plan. The roof lines are then drawn. You now have a framework which is used as an underlay for sketches.

D. Lay a piece of yellow tracing paper over the framework and make sketches trying different window locations. You can also make interior sketches or try different roof lines.

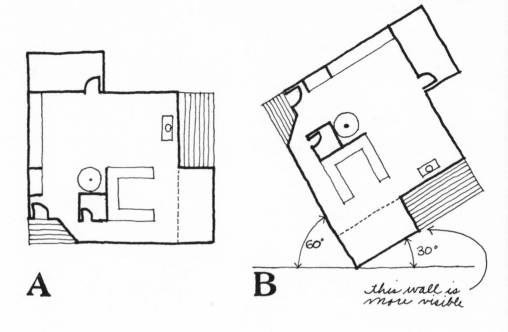

A

B

this wall is more visible

60° 30°

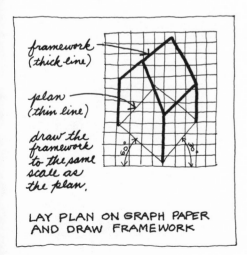

framework (thick line)

plan (thin line)

draw the framework to the same scale as the plan.

LAY PLAN ON GRAPH PAPER AND DRAW FRAMEWORK

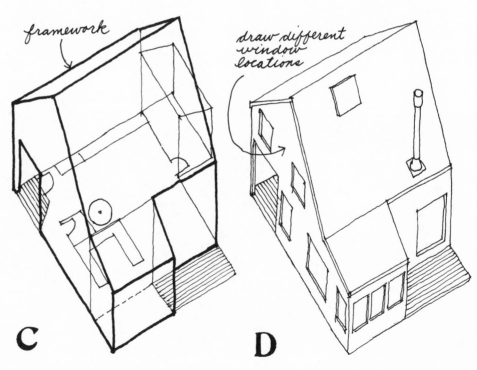

framework

draw different window locations

C

D

71

8. Study Models

The next step is to make a paper or cardboard study model. These are used to explore shapes, inside space, and light.

There are two types of study models which will be helpful in your designing. The first type is the small mass model. Mass models are, as the name implies, to study the overall shape or massing and if you want to study the basic window arrangement or "fenestration." They are easy to make and are usually made to the scale of one-eighth inch equals one foot.

They are made out of lightweight strathmore or tag board (or even shirt cardboard). They can be easily made by cutting, scoring, and folding as shown here.

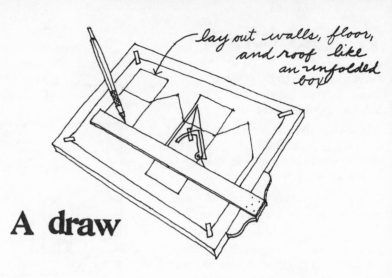

lay out walls, floor, and roof like an unfolded box

A draw

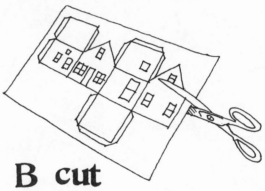

B cut

use a dry ball point pen or similar blunt tool to score the fold lines.

C score

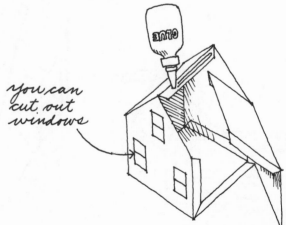

you can cut out windows

D fold & glue

72

mass model

To get an idea of how to make a mass
model, cut out the model and put it
together as shown here.

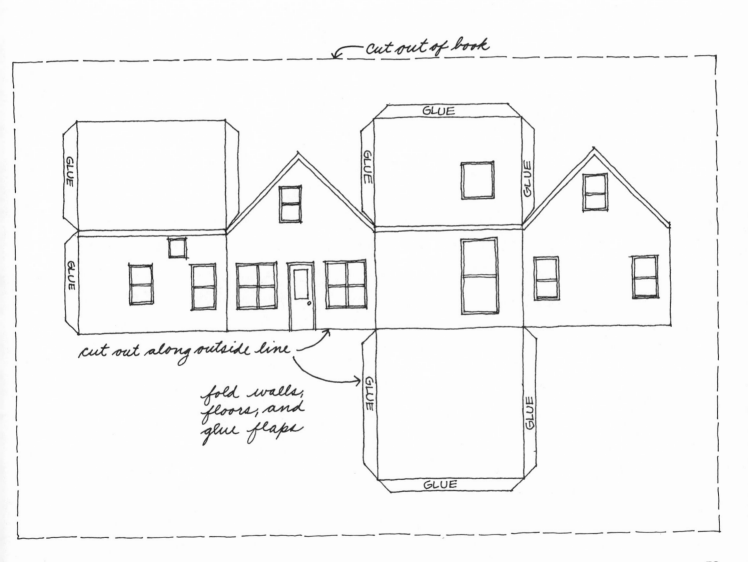

cut out of book

GLUE

GLUE

GLUE

GLUE

GLUE

GLUE

GLUE

GLUE

cut out along outside line

fold walls,
floors, and
glue flaps

Here are two mass models made by Fred and Lois to study different roof configurations. One is a shed roof and the other is a gable roof. Fred and Lois decide that they like the gable roof best. This allows for an attic space to be used for studios. It also allows for an opening skylight which takes advantage of the stack effect for natural ventilation.

Fred and Lois make several plan sketches from their bubble diagram and decide that they like the plan shown in drawing number 1. It is basically a simple large shape with two levels and a two-story high space in the living room. The entry porch, the shop, and the dining space are forms outside the main space, while the bathroom and kitchen are like rooms within the main space. The stairs have been located but they are not yet right (architects say "it isn't working") because they waste space on the second floor. The circulation is open and free because there are no corridors. Lois likes the kitchen open to the rest of the house as shown. Her studio is a separate structure outside the house.

There are deciduous trees on the south and west sides which will provide summer shade while allowing winter sun to warm the house.

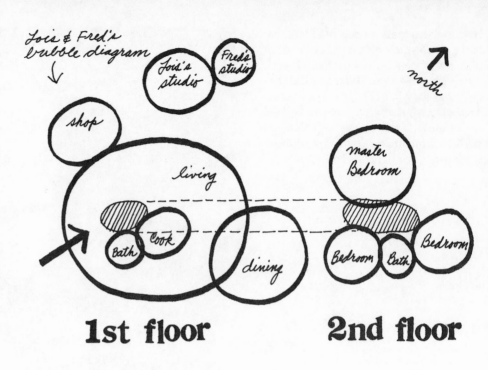

1st floor **2nd floor**

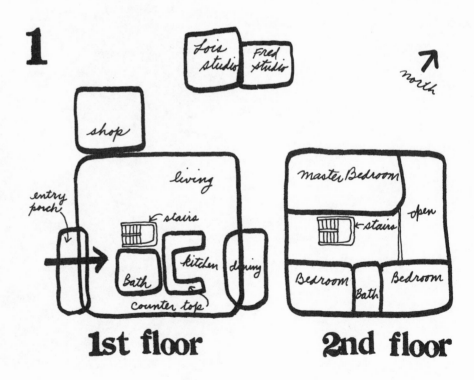

1st floor **2nd floor**

In drawing number 2 the plan is developed further. Doors, closets, and fixtures are shown. An outdoor porch has been added. A new stair design has been tried, but it still does not work. It takes up too much space and is not accessible to the entry.

At this point Fred and Lois decide to do a rough cost estimate on what they have drawn. They have asked some local contractors and found that houses using the kind of materials they want to use for building are going for about $25.00 per square foot in their area. This is a rough figure, since many factors enter into the cost. Unusual problems such as water or sewage can be disasterous. Also, a small house will cost more per square foot since certain costs are fixed, such as kitchen, bath, well and septic system (if needed).

Fred and Lois give dimensions to the plan and add up the square feet. It comes to 1,720 square feet. They multiply by $25.00 per square foot; this comes out to $43,000.

This is too much money, since their program says $35,000 is the limit. The house must be cut. There are many ways to cut costs. Eliminate rooms, make rooms smaller, use cheaper materials, etc.

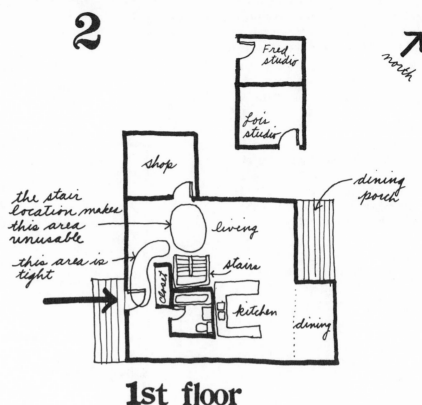

2

north

Fred studio

Lois studio

shop

the stair location makes this area unusable

this area is tight

living

dining porch

stairs

Closet

kitchen

dining

1st floor

FLOOR AREA:
first floor = 860 square ft.
studios = 140 square ft.
second floor = 720 square ft.

TOTAL = 1720 square ft.
multiply → $25/square ft
COST = $43,000

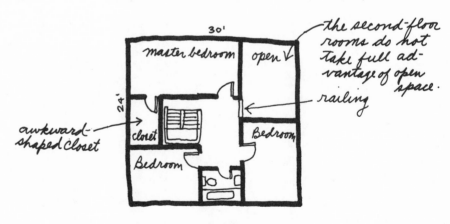

30'

master bedroom

open ↓

the second-floor rooms do not take full advantage of open space.

24'

railing

awkward-shaped closet

closet

Bedroom

Bedroom

2nd floor

Fred and Lois decide to drop the entry porch in favor of a small entry alcove, to try to fit Lois's studio into the house and to make the overall size of the house smaller.

A circular stair is tried and this seems to work well. It is decided that a third level will be added to accommodate Fred and Lois's studios. Going up is generally cheaper than adding on at ground level since you don't need additional foundation. The master bedroom is shifted to the middle which allows the children's rooms to open to below with sliding panels.

The orientation of the house allows summer breezes to draw air out of the house, and the children's bedrooms are protected from winter winds.

They make cut-out pieces of furniture and place them in all the rooms to make sure that the room sizes are adequate and the doors and windows are correctly placed.

This drawing is made to the scale of one-quarter inch equals one foot, zero inches. It is shown in drawing number 3.

3

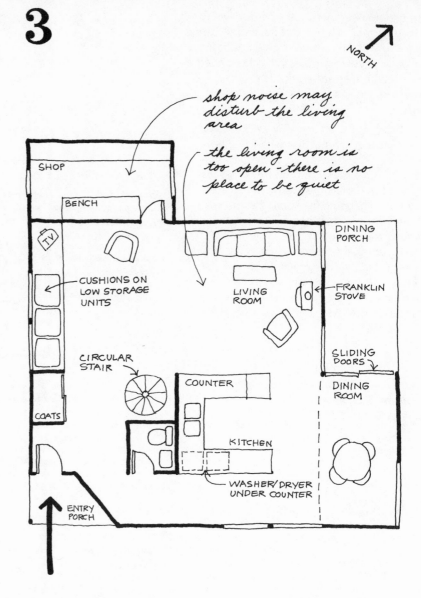

shop noise may disturb the living area

the living room is too open - there is no place to be quiet

NORTH

SHOP
BENCH
TV
CUSHIONS ON LOW STORAGE UNITS
CIRCULAR STAIR
COATS
ENTRY PORCH
COUNTER
KITCHEN
WASHER/DRYER UNDER COUNTER
LIVING ROOM
DINING PORCH
FRANKLIN STOVE
SLIDING DOORS
DINING ROOM

1st floor

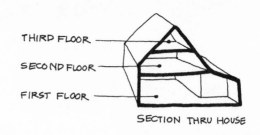

SECTION THRU HOUSE

THIRD FLOOR
SECOND FLOOR
FIRST FLOOR

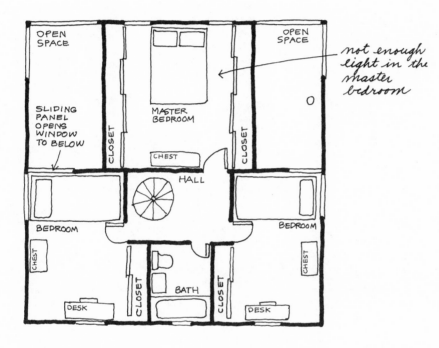

OPEN SPACE

OPEN SPACE

not enough light in the master bedroom

SLIDING PANEL OPENS WINDOW TO BELOW

MASTER BEDROOM

CLOSET

CHEST

CLOSET

HALL

BEDROOM

BEDROOM

CHEST

CHEST

DESK

CLOSET

BATH

CLOSET

DESK

2nd floor

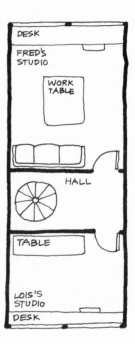

DESK

FRED'S STUDIO

WORK TABLE

HALL

TABLE

LOIS'S STUDIO

DESK

3rd floor

corrugated cardboard models

Fred and Lois now decide to build a large-scale rough model to study the inside space and light. These models are best made at a scale of three-eighth inches or one-half inch equals one foot using corrugated cardboard, recycled from large corrugated cardboard boxes. The large scale allows you to study the light and space by putting your eye right down into the spaces.

You will be amazed at how similar the experience is to actually being in the space if you let your imagination go.

Here is how to make a large-scale corrugated model.

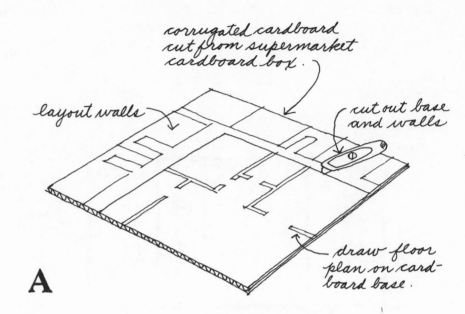

corrugated cardboard
cut from supermarket
cardboard box.

layout walls

cut out base
and walls

draw floor
plan on card-
board base.

A

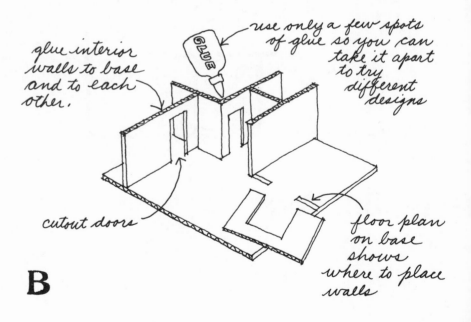

glue interior
walls to base
and to each
other.

use only a few spots
of glue so you can
take it apart
to try
different
designs

GLUE

cutout doors

floor plan
on base
shows
where to place
walls

B

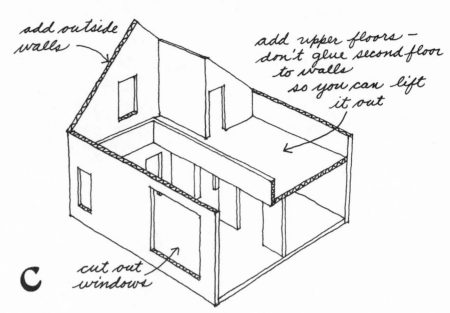

add outside walls

add upper floors — don't glue second floor to walls so you can lift it out

cut out windows

C

by placing your cardboard model on your land on a sunny day, the sun angles can be observed. all the shadows will be in proportion to the future real house shadows.

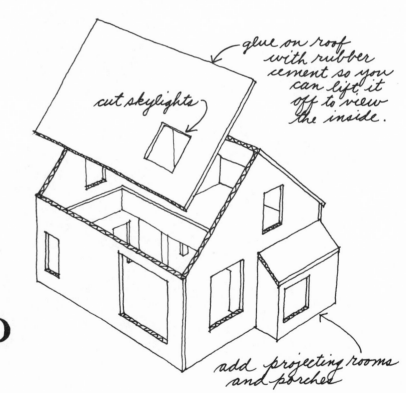

glue on roof with rubber cement so you can lift it off to view the inside.

cut skylights

D

add projecting rooms and porches

Shown here is the sequence of Fred and Lois building their corrugated cardboard model.

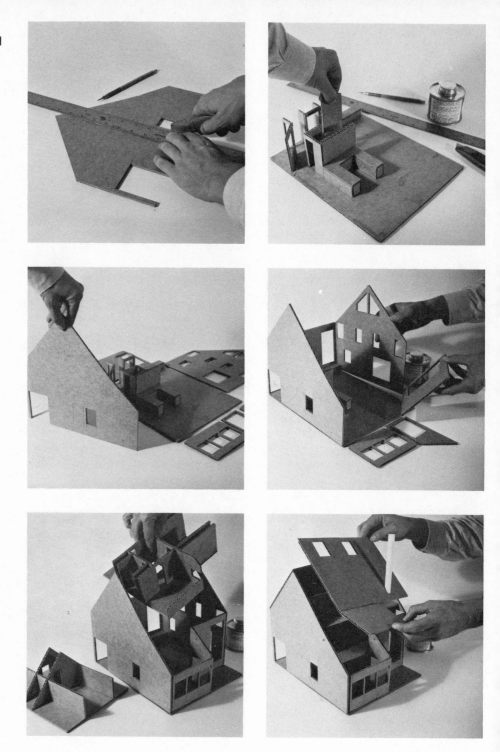

Below is Fred and Lois's corrugated model showing the first floor. They have studied the inside and decide that the living room can be better used if it is divided into quiet and noisy areas. A sliding door is designed to achieve this.

Below, Fred and Lois have inserted the second floor into the model and have discovered that Phoebe's bedroom can be made to overlook the kitchen. This will allow them to keep contact with Phoebe.

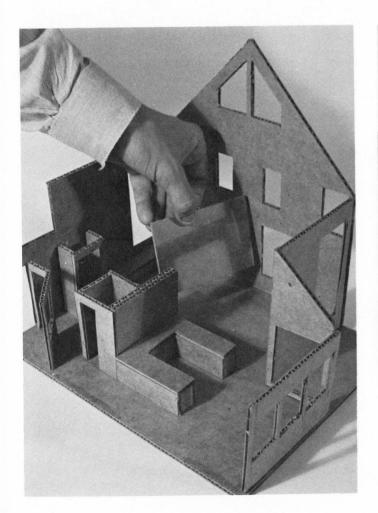

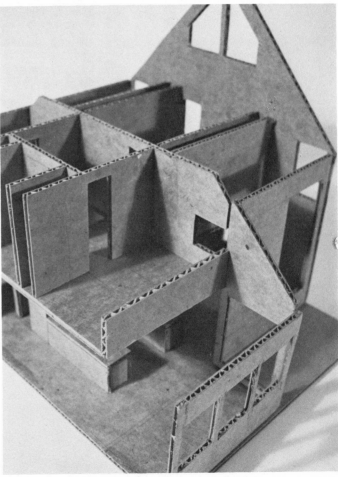

Next, Fred and Lois cut out skylights on the northeast side of the roof for their studios, to allow for indirect light for most of the day. A skylight is also cut over the stair. A lean-to greenhouse is tried on the south side for Lois's plants. This will be an added expense but they decide it is worth it, since Lois loves to grow unusual plants.

A curved window in the third-story space is tried for fun. The shop is pulled away from the house to eliminate noise.

84

The model is now placed on a large piece
of white paper and the site is sketched at
an appropriate size so that views, sun,
shade, and breezes can be checked.

Necessary changes are made.

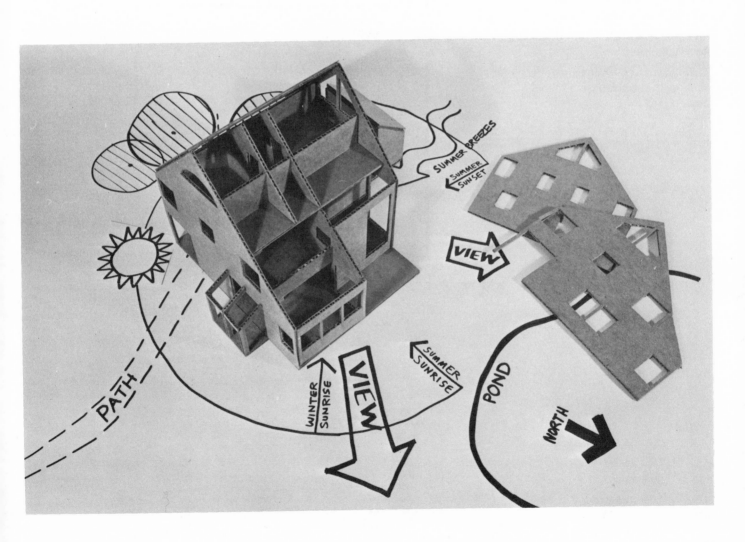

9. Final Plan

At this point go back and put all the changes you made in your models and sketches into a final plan drawing. Shown here is Fred and Lois's final plan.

They have decided to use a sliding glass door to close off the greenhouse during the winter, to save heat loss.

They have inserted in their drawing the sliding barn door that separates the living room into noisy and quiet areas.

The shop is separated from the main house.

The final window arrangement determined with the corrugated model is shown.

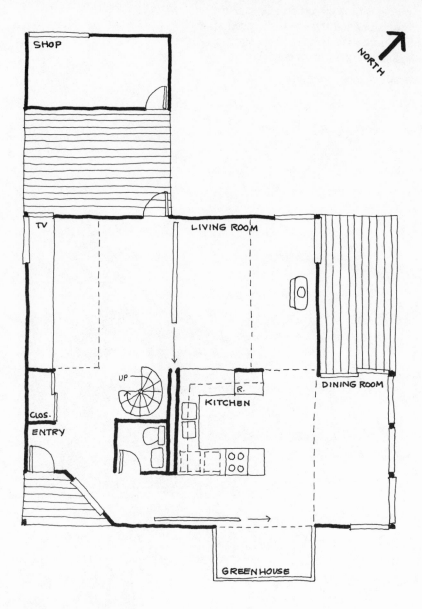

1st floor

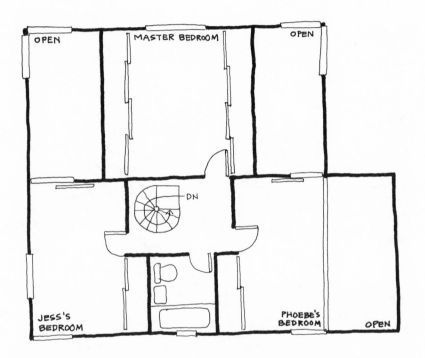

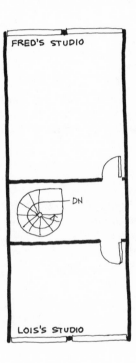

2nd floor

3rd floor

10. Finish Models

The second type of model is a detailed finish model called so because it is to study finishes such as wall textures and colors.

It is the last step in design (before construction drawings). Take the corrugated cardboard model and cut out color paper walls. Try out different combinations. See how a change in one wall color affects all the others. You can also make window frames and facia boards out of small basswood strips. Using rubber cement, change the model until you find the combination you like best.

The drawing shows some other things you can do to finish the model.

Basswood (and other model building materials) is available from hobby shops. It is used to build model railroad towns.

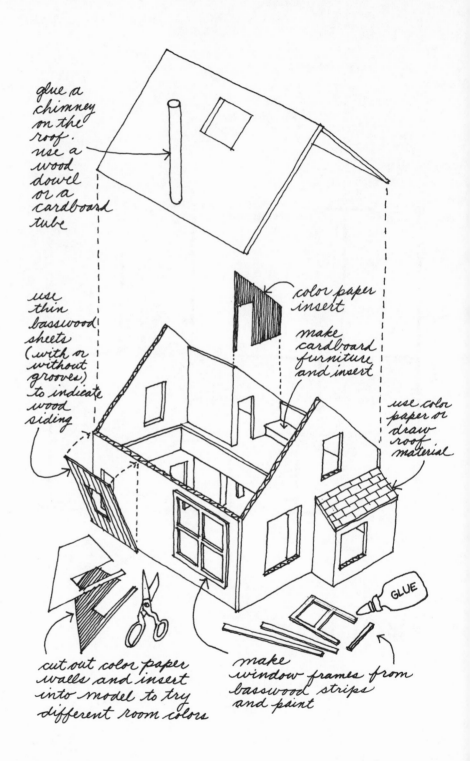

glue a chimney on the roof. use a wood dowel or a cardboard tube

use thin basswood sheets (with or without grooves) to indicate wood siding

color paper insert

make cardboard furniture and insert

use color paper or draw roof material

cut out color paper walls and insert into model to try different room colors

make window frames from basswood strips and paint

GLUE

Here is a photograph of Fred and Lois's
corrugated model being used to study
interior room colors.

4. Preparing Construction Drawings

Preparing a set of construction drawings is one of those tasks that seems impossible at first, especially if you've never drawn. But if you start at the beginning and go one simple step at a time, you'll find that you can do it! This final chapter is devoted to teaching you how to make the drawings that are necessary to get your house built. We start by showing you what construction drawings are, then how to set up and begin. Next we give you three easy steps (drawing-dimensioning-labeling) for producing a set of drawings. Follow them and you'll see how easy and how much fun it is to develop your design on paper. We complete the chapter with a happy ending to the Fred and Lois story - a completed set of drawings of their house, ready to build.

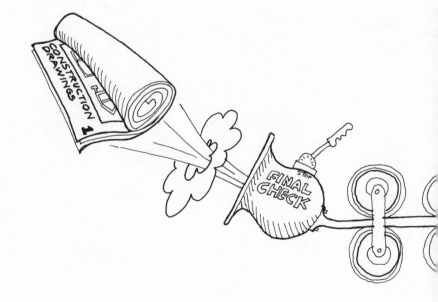

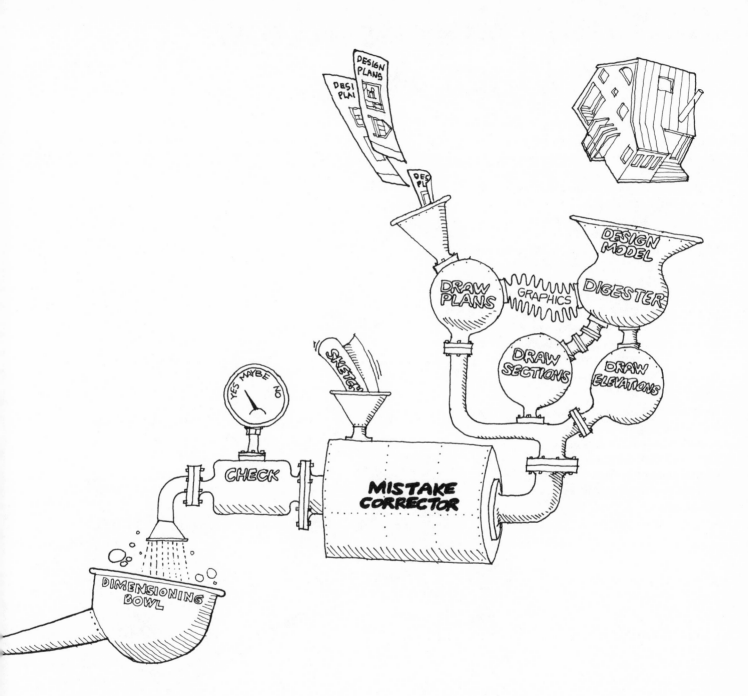

A. What Construction Drawings Are

Construction drawings can be described as a simple graphic representation of all the decisions that you've made since you began designing a home with bubble diagrams. The amount of work that you put into your drawings will depend, in part, on the amount of information the builder needs. Find a builder you can trust and meet with him before you start your drawings. If you plan to build the house yourself, you can draw as you build. In any case, we want to stress that these drawings are just *tools to communicate your ideas to the builder* (room size, door, window and fixture locations, materials, ceiling heights, and anything else that might come up) - you decide how complex they need to be.

A set of construction drawings usually includes the following four kinds of drawings: Floor Plans, Sections, Elevations, and Sketch Details. The next five pages will describe these drawings; then we'll show you how to do your set.

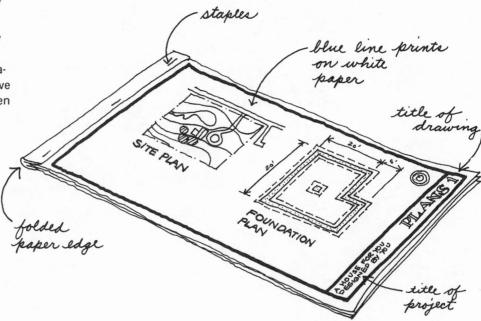

staples

blue line prints on white paper

title of drawing

SITE PLAN

FOUNDATION PLAN

PLANS 1

A HOUSE FOR YOU DESIGNED BY YOU

folded paper edge

title of project

plans

The *floor plan* is a bird's-eye view of a particular floor level of your house after an imaginary horizontal cut is made through the house walls and the top of the house is lifted away. The first-floor plan (a horizontal cut through the first-floor walls) shows the first floor. The second-floor plan (a horizontal cut through the second-floor walls) shows the second floor, and so on. Floor plans are perhaps the most important drawings in the set since they show the builder the exact size and outline of the house, as well as the locations of every wall, door, window, fixture, electric outlets, built-in furniture, and other proposed interior construction.

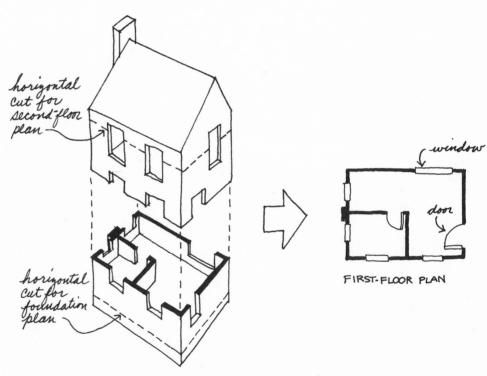

horizontal cut for second-floor plan

horizontal cut for foundation plan

window

door

FIRST-FLOOR PLAN

The *site plan* is a bird's-eye view of all of your land shown as it will look after your house is built. Its purpose is to show the builder the proposed location of your house on your land as well as the location of other proposed exterior construction, such as the driveway, walks, and landscaping areas.

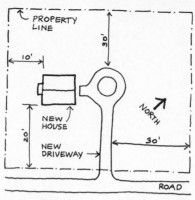

SITE PLAN

The *framing plan* is a bird's-eye view of just the structural lumber of a particular floor level. Its purpose is to show the builder how to build, or "frame," that floor.

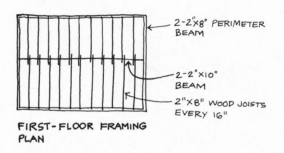

FIRST-FLOOR FRAMING PLAN

The *foundation plan* is a bird's-eye view of the foundation of your house after an imaginary, horizontal cut is made through the foundation walls and the rest of the house is lifted away. The purpose of this plan is to show the builder the exact location and type of foundation to be used to support your house.

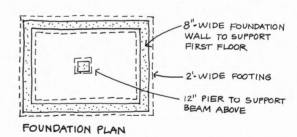

FOUNDATION PLAN

sections

The *section* is a view of your house after making an imaginary verticle cut through the entire building. The purpose of this cutaway drawing is to show how high floors and ceilings are above the first-floor level and how deep the foundations go into the ground. It also gives detailed information, such as the size of framing lumber, size of foundation, and type of interior siding and flooring materials. A complicated design may require a number of sections, but usually two (a North-South cut and an East-West cut) are adequate.

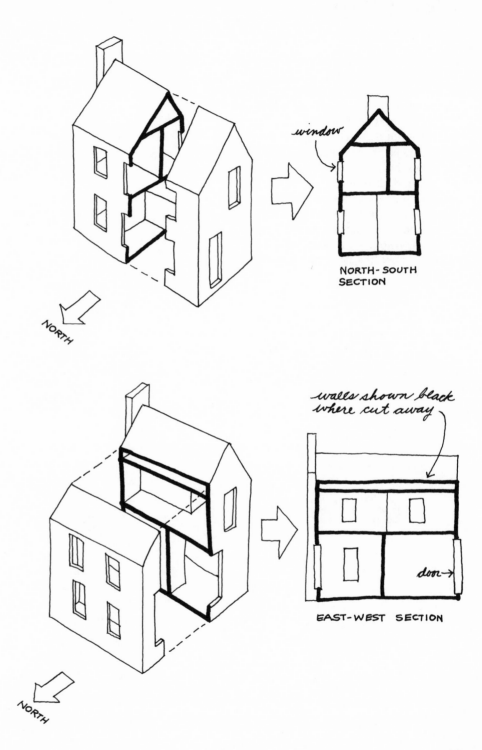

window

NORTH-SOUTH SECTION

NORTH

walls shown black where cut away

door →

EAST-WEST SECTION

NORTH

95

elevations

Elevations are straight-on views of your house, taken from the N, S, E, and W. They are usually labeled according to the direction they face. Thus, the North Elevation faces north, and so on. When plans are not designed for a specific location, they can be labeled front, rear, left side, and right side. Their purpose is to show the kinds of materials used on the exterior walls and roof, and to designate the style (and usually the manufacturer) of exterior windows and doors. Sometimes the heights of windows above a floor level and the slope of the roof are given here.

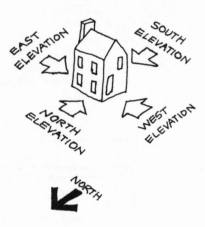

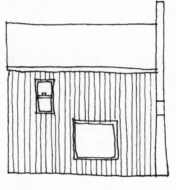

SOUTH ELEVATION

EAST ELEVATION

WEST ELEVATION

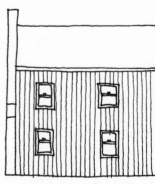

NORTH ELEVATION

sketch details

We are including *sketches* here because it will probably be the easiest way for you to convey to the builder detailed information of special places in your house that you're not quite sure how to draw. They might include drawings of stairs, kitchen cabinets, special built-in furniture, or just an idea you might have regarding a skylight or a fireplace. Architects call these drawings "details."

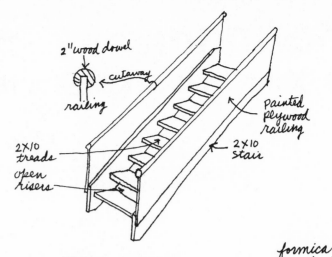

2" wood dowel

cutaway

railing

2×10 treads

open risers

painted plywood railing

2×10 stair

FIRST-FLOOR STAIR

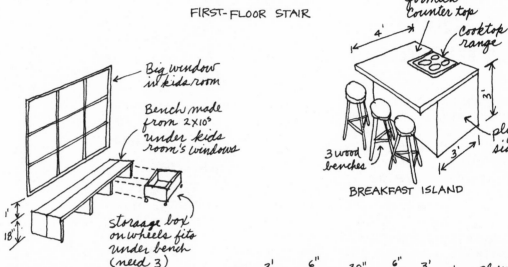

Big window in kids room

Bench made from 2×10s under kids room's windows

1'

18"

storage box on wheels fits under bench (need 3)

KID'S STORAGE BENCH

formica counter top

cooktop range

4'

3'

3 wood benches

3'

plywood sides

BREAKFAST ISLAND

The amount of detail that you need in these sketches, of course, depends greatly on your relationship with the builder. For example, he may be able to build a satisfactory set of built-in shelves after you've just pointed out their location. Or, he may want exact drawings regarding the height, width, and depth of each shelf, how they are supported, and their exact location.

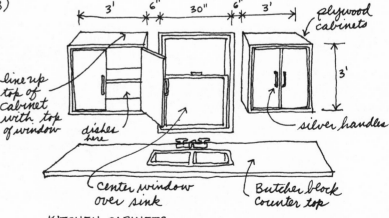

3'   6"   30"   6"   3'

plywood cabinets

line up top of cabinet with top of window

dishes here

3'

silver handles

center window over sink

Butcher block counter top

KITCHEN CABINETS

B. Beginning
Getting Your Drawings Started

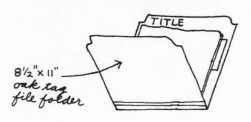

8½" × 11" oak tag file folder

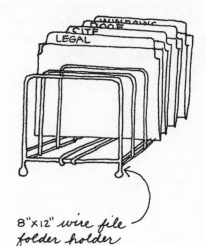

8" × 12" wire file folder holder

1. Gather Information

Now is the time to start filling your head with the details of all the materials and fixtures that you will want in your design. It is critical that you spend as much time as possible at home improvement centers, hardware stores, and lumber yards, teaching yourself about all the various materials that are available to you. Pay particular attention to interior and exterior cladding materials since they will play a big role in the overall "aesthetic" of your house in general, and each room in particular. Find out what kind of kitchen and bathroom fixtures are available. Get all the various manufacturers' catalogs and brochures to help you make decisions. Get prices (usually not in catalogs) on everything.

In order for you and your builder to have quick, easy access to this information, you should begin a file system.

Make a file with titles as follows:

1. Legal (permits and contracts, etc.)
2. Site - septic and driveway, etc.
3. Framing - special braces, notes, etc.
4. Roof
5. Windows and doors (skylights and greenhouses)
6. Exterior wall materials and finishes (paint, etc.)
7. Interior wall, floor, and ceiling materials
8. Stairs and interior trim
9. Kitchen and bathroom fixtures and plumbing
10. Lighting and electrical
11. Heating systems and fireplaces, wood-burning stoves, and solar
12. Cabinets (kitchen and bath) and other built-in furniture
13. Hardware

2. Give Yourself a Crash Course in Building Construction

If you spend just a few hours reading one of the good housebuilding books such as Blackburne's *Illustrated Housebuilding* or *Modern Carpentry*, you'll begin to understand important basic building construction principles that are crucial in the development of your set of drawings. Again, keep in mind the idea that construction drawings are the graphic representation of all the decisions you've made. The more you know about building construction techniques and the materials available to you, the better your decisions will be.

The following is a brief listing of key methods and materials that you will need. This listing is to acquaint you with building construction. You should research each category carefully, by reading and by talking with local builders and homeowners, before making your final choice.

footings & foundations

The foundation's job is to support the weight of the house. The footing is the part of the foundation that spreads out at the base to form a "foot" or pad that keeps the house from sinking.

Basically, there are two types of foundations: pier foundations and continuous foundations.

The *pier type* is a series of columns or legs that go into the ground, resting on footings, to support the building.

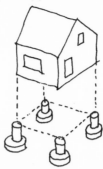

The *continuous type* is a perimeter wall around the bottom of the house, resting on footings, to support the building.

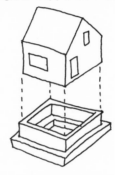

The pier type is usually the least expensive (using the least materials and labor). It is used extensively for cabins, sheds, and small houses, and is good for steep slopes and areas where you don't want to disturb what is under the house (plants or stream, etc.). The continuous type is the most common house foundation. It is good for insulation, provides a crawl space or basement, and can be used in all types of soil (it distributes the load of the house over a large area).

Here are some common pier and continuous foundations. Choose one after consulting with your builder, homeowners in your neighborhood, and anyone else who might help regarding snow loads and soil conditions.

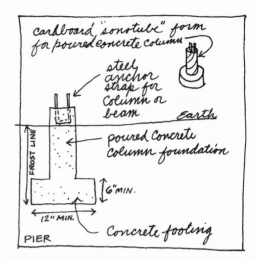

cardboard "sonotube" form for poured concrete column

steel anchor strap for column or beam

Earth

poured concrete column foundation

6" MIN.

12" MIN.

Concrete footing

PIER

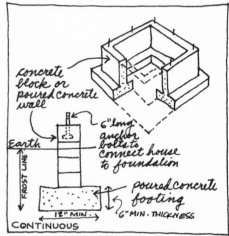

concrete block or poured concrete wall

Earth

6" long anchor bolts to connect house to foundation

poured concrete footing

6" MIN. THICKNESS

12" MIN.

CONTINUOUS

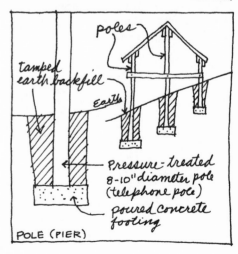

poles

tamped earth backfill

Earth

Pressure-treated 8-10" diameter pole (telephone pole)

poured concrete footing

POLE (PIER)

framing

The frame is the structural part of the house. It provides support for floor, walls, and ceiling materials.

There are two types of framing in use today: plank and beam frame and 2x4 stud platform frame.

Plank and beam was the primary way that houses and barns were framed 150 years ago. This system employs large, thick, heavy pieces of wood and requires a crew of builders to erect.

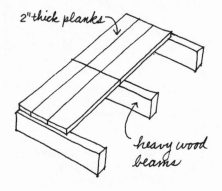

2" thick planks

heavy wood beams

Plank and beam is still common in homes where exposed beams in ceilings are desired. It resists fire well.

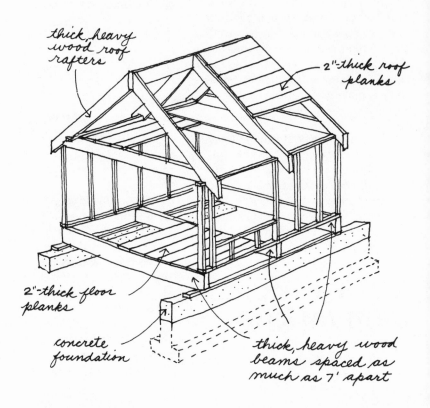

thick, heavy wood roof rafters

2"-thick roof planks

2"-thick floor planks

concrete foundation

thick, heavy wood beams spaced as much as 7' apart

PLANK AND BEAM FRAME

Platform framing is used in most residential construction today. The first floor is built on the foundation as though it were a "platform." This provides a base upon which the carpenter can build walls which he eventually tilts up into place. Then another, second-floor platform is built on those walls, and so on. This system uses very light, small pieces of wood (2x4 in the walls), used repetitively.

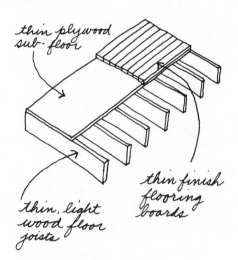

thin plywood sub-floor

thin finish flooring boards

thin, light wood floor joists

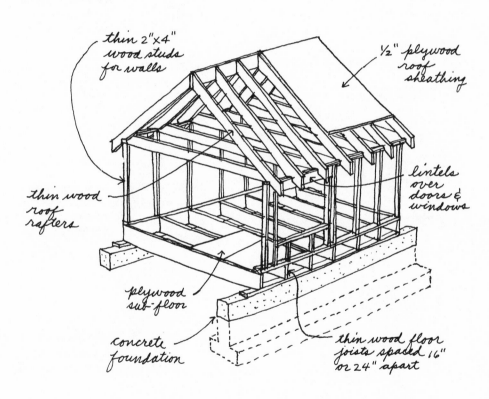

thin 2"x4" wood studs for walls

½" plywood roof sheathing

thin wood roof rafters

lintels over doors & windows

plywood sub-floor

concrete foundation

thin wood floor joists spaced 16" or 24" apart

PLATFORM FRAME

windows

Windows allow light and fresh air into your home, so they are one of the most important parts you will have to consider. There are three basic types of windows: sliding, swinging, and fixed. Each of these comes in a wide variety of sizes. Metal factory sash windows are an inexpensive way of creating a large windowed area.

When locating windows in the walls of your design try to imagine yourself in the room, looking out. Remember to take advantage of views, of direct sunlight, and of north light.

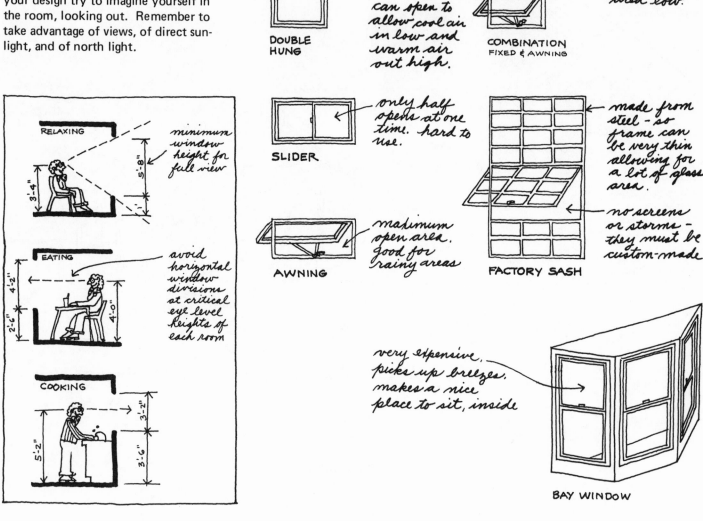

FIXED — custom-made. no moving parts. no ventilation. used for views

CASEMENT — inexpensive- used to catch breezes — maximum open area

DOUBLE HUNG — most inexpensive. only half opens at one time. can open to allow cool air in low and warm air out high.

COMBINATION FIXED & AWNING — viewing area up high and ventilation area low.

SLIDER — only half opens at one time. hard to use.

AWNING — maximum open area. good for rainy areas

FACTORY SASH — made from steel - so frame can be very thin allowing for a lot of glass area. — no screens or storms - they must be custom-made

RELAXING — minimum window height for full view — 3'-4" — 5'-8"

EATING — 2'-6" — 4'-2" — 4'-0" — avoid horizontal window divisions at critical eye level heights of each room

COOKING — 5'-2" — 3'-2" — 3'-6"

BAY WINDOW — very expensive. picks up breezes. makes a nice place to sit, inside

doors

Doors are moving parts in constant use and therefore need to be well made and installed properly. When considering doors, you must think of insect control, snow and rain protection, and heat loss. Doors are usually 6'-8" high by various widths from 2'-0" to 3'-6". Most exterior doors are 6'-8" by 3'-0" and most interior doors are 6'-8" by 2'-0" to 2'-6". They are usually made and brought to the site in their frame.

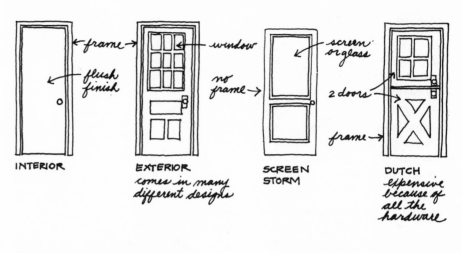

INTERIOR

EXTERIOR
comes in many different designs

SCREEN STORM

DUTCH
expensive because of all the hardware

frame · flush finish · window · no frame · screen or glass · 2 doors · frame

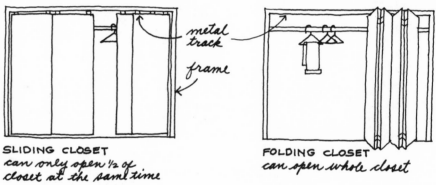

SLIDING CLOSET
can only open ½ of closet at the same time

FOLDING CLOSET
can open whole closet

metal track · frame

You may want to open a complete wall of your house to include the outside in the summer. Here are 2 doors that can be used for this purpose.

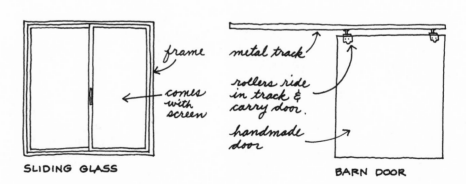

SLIDING GLASS

BARN DOOR

frame · comes with screen · metal track · rollers ride in track & carry door · handmade door

103

roofing

Roofing is the material that will comprise one of the primary visible exterior surfaces of your house, so care should be taken in its selection. Color and texture must be considered with cost, ability to resist fire, and longevity.

For flat roofs and low sloping roofs, a watertight layer must be constructed. This is done by laminating roofing felts with asphalt or coal tar pitch and then covering that surface with crushed stone.

Materials for sloping roofs include asphalt roll roofing, asphalt, wood shingles, tile, galvanized sheet metal, aluminum sheets, and translucent fiber glass sheets.

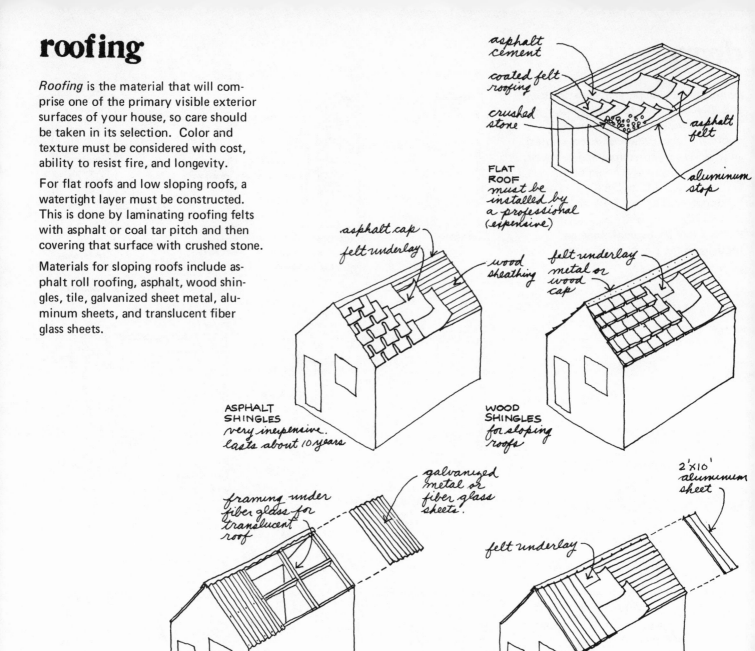

asphalt cement
coated felt roofing
crushed stone
asphalt felt
aluminum stop

FLAT ROOF *must be installed by a professional (expensive)*

asphalt cap
felt underlay
wood sheathing

felt underlay
metal or wood cap

ASPHALT SHINGLES *very inexpensive. lasts about 10 years*

WOOD SHINGLES *for sloping roofs*

framing under fiber glass for translucent roof

galvanized metal or fiber glass sheets.

2'x10' aluminum sheet

felt underlay

CORRUGATED *easy to install. needs no underlayment.*

ALUMINUM *expensive but lasts 30 years or more*

exterior wall cladding

Exterior wall cladding is the finish material that is attached to the frame to weatherproof the walls. The choice of this material is important and since it is the major exterior surface, it will set the tone for the outside aesthetic.

Usually all of the walls of a framed house are covered with a layer of ½" unsanded plywood - commonly called sheathing. This sheathing adds much strength to the structure and provides a nailing surface for the finish material. A layer of tar paper is usually stapled over the sheathing for extra protection before the finish material is installed.

Wood shingles are available in a wide range of sizes and colors. A visit to your local lumber yard will suggest what is readily available.

Mineral fiber shingles, also called asbestos cement siding, are factory-made shingles with prefinished baked coatings. They are also available in a variety of textures and colors.

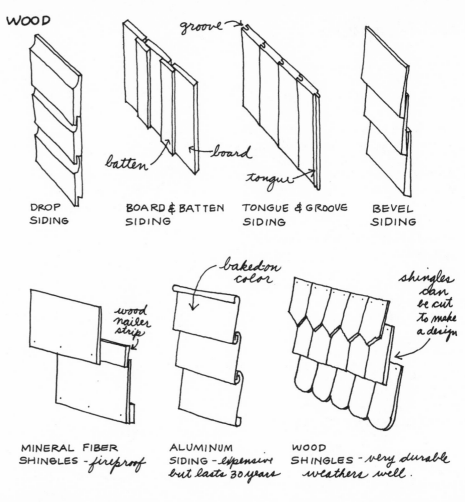

WOOD

DROP SIDING

BOARD & BATTEN SIDING — batten — board

TONGUE & GROOVE SIDING — groove — tongue

BEVEL SIDING

MINERAL FIBER SHINGLES - *fireproof* — wood nailer strip

ALUMINUM SIDING - *expensive but lasts 30 years* — baked on color

WOOD SHINGLES - *very durable weathers well.* — shingles can be cut to make a design

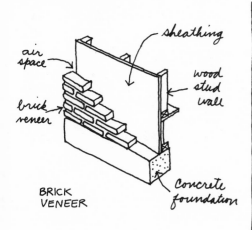

BRICK VENEER — sheathing, air space, brick veneer, wood stud wall, concrete foundation

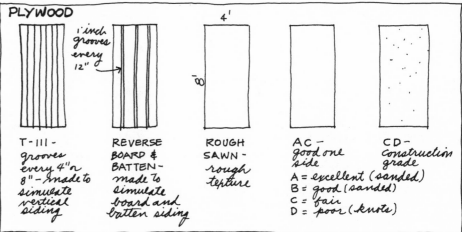

PLYWOOD

T-III - grooves every 4" or 8" - made to simulate vertical siding

REVERSE BOARD & BATTEN - made to simulate board and batten siding — 1 inch grooves every 12"

ROUGH SAWN - rough texture — 4'

AC - good one side

CD - construction grade

A = excellent (sanded)
B = good (sanded)
C = fair
D = poor (knots)

insulation

Insulation is the blanket of material that surrounds the house to keep in heated or cooled air. There are many different types of insulation all having a rating that tells you the ability of the insulating material to resist the flow of heat. This rating is called the R-value. Every element of a wall, floor, or ceiling - even air spaces - that you include in your design has an R-value. Add together the various R-values in a wall, floor, or ceiling and you get its total thermal resistance.

3½" BLANKET FIBER GLASS used in walls — 15" or 23" wide to fit between studs

6" BATT FIBER GLASS used in floors and ceilings — 15" or 23" wide to fit between floor joists and roof rafters

For a typical frame house wall:

	R
Wood Siding	.81
Wood sheathing	1.32
3½" fiber gl. insul.	11.00
½" wallboard	.45
air film next to outside wall	.17
air film next to inside wall	.68
Total R	14.43

A representative of your local electric company can tell you what R-value you should design to in floors, ceilings, and walls (usually floors and ceilings are insulated twice as much as walls) in your locale. In the example above if the standard R-design for the wall was 12.00, the wall would be well insulated.

The various types of insulation are shown here. The R-values are always marked on the insulation package.

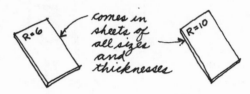

1" RIGID STYRENE — comes in sheets of all sizes and thicknesses

1" RIGID URETHANE

these 2 types of insulation can be used on the outside of the roof sheathing (under finished roof) so that the roof rafters can be exposed.

LOOSE FILL vermiculite or other granulated material — poured between studs, joists and rafters after the interior and exterior wall cladding has been installed.

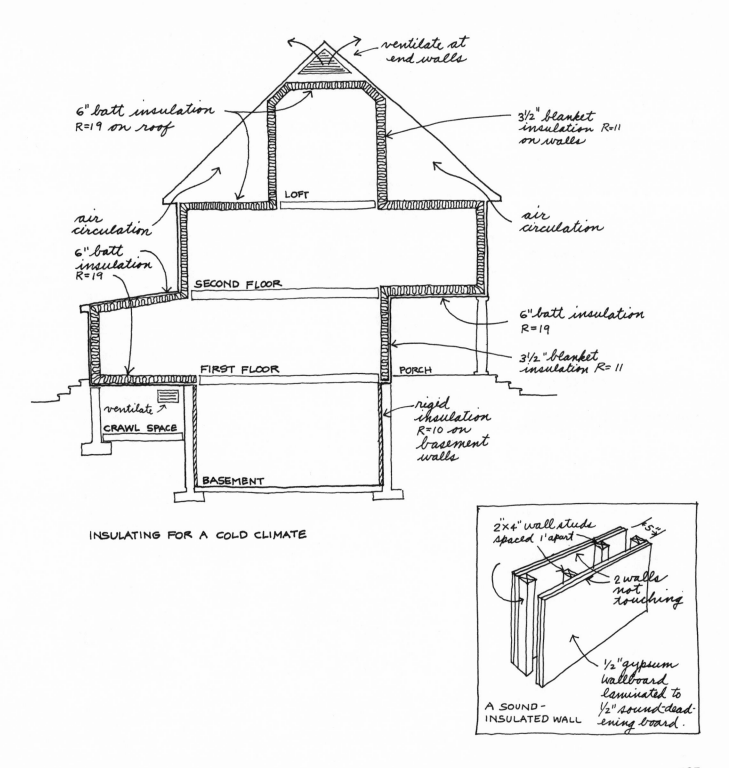

ventilate at end walls

6" batt insulation R=19 on roof

3½" blanket insulation R=11 on walls

LOFT

air circulation

air circulation

6" batt insulation R=19

SECOND FLOOR

6" batt insulation R=19

3½" blanket insulation R=11

FIRST FLOOR

PORCH

rigid insulation R=10 on basement walls

ventilate

CRAWL SPACE

BASEMENT

INSULATING FOR A COLD CLIMATE

2"x4" wall studs spaced 1' apart

5"

2 walls not touching

½" gypsum wallboard laminated to ½" sound-deadening board.

A SOUND-INSULATED WALL

interior wall cladding

Interior wall cladding can be almost any material since they do not have to resist the weather. Listed are a few of the most common ones, but this is one area in which you can freely use your imagination.

Sheetrock, gypsum board, or drywall, commonly called wallboard, are 4'x8' sheets of paper covered gypsum that are nailed to the studs. Then the nail holes and joints are smoothly covered and finished with a putty substance so that the finish resembles plaster.

Solid wood paneling is an attractive and durable wall surface available in many different kinds of wood and patterns.

skylights & greenhouses

Skylights always add special touches by admitting light, and sometimes air, through the roof of your house.

Greenhouses are used for growing plants and should face south for that purpose. They can also be used to open up a large area of wall to a view that might be upward oriented.

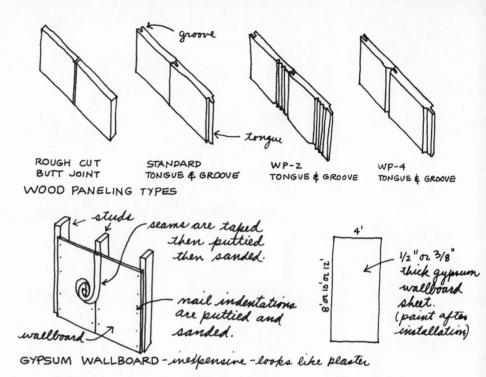

ROUGH CUT BUTT JOINT

STANDARD TONGUE & GROOVE

WP-2 TONGUE & GROOVE

WP-4 TONGUE & GROOVE

WOOD PANELING TYPES

groove

tongue

studs — seams are taped then puttied then sanded.

nail indentations are puttied and sanded.

wallboard

4'

1/2" or 3/8" thick gypsum wallboard sheet. (paint after installation)

8', 10', or 12'

GYPSUM WALLBOARD - *inexpensive - looks like plaster*

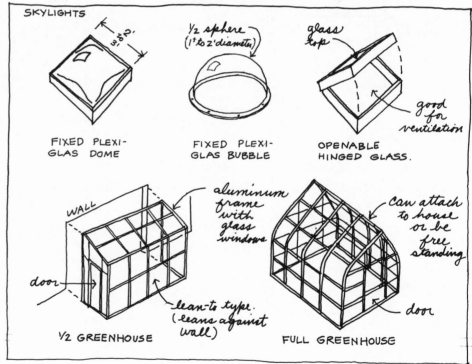

SKYLIGHTS

3', 2'

1/2 sphere (1' to 2' diameter)

glass top

good for ventilation

FIXED PLEXI-GLAS DOME

FIXED PLEXI-GLAS BUBBLE

OPENABLE HINGED GLASS.

WALL

aluminum frame with glass windows

can attach to house or be free standing

door

lean-to type. (leans against wall)

door

1/2 GREENHOUSE

FULL GREENHOUSE

heating

There are several different heating systems that can be installed in your house, depending on climate, your budget, and the amount of time and energy you wish to spend.

The cast iron stove or wood-burning stove is very inexpensive to install and to operate. However, it requires a lot of time and energy chopping wood and stoking the fire.

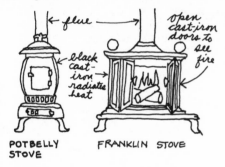

POTBELLY STOVE

FRANKLIN STOVE

The kerosene heater is very inexpensive to operate (fuel costs are low) but it can be a fire hazard and will cause soot.

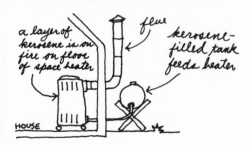

KEROSENE SPACE HEATER

Electric heat (baseboard) is the least expensive automatic heating system to install but the most expensive to operate although each room can be controlled separately, saving money. Electric heat is very dry and sometimes uncomfortable.

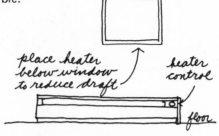

place heater below window to reduce draft

heater control

floor

ELECTRIC BASEBOARD HEATER

Hot water heat is the most expensive system to install but it gives off the most comfortable heat (it doesn't take the humidity from the air). This system requires a furnace to heat the water and a series of baseboard units, connected by water pipes.

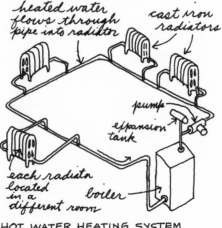

heated water flows through pipe into radiator

cast iron radiators

pump

expansion tank

each radiator located in a different room

boiler

HOT WATER HEATING SYSTEM (one pipe)

Hot air heat is fairly expensive to install and can be noisy. It requires a furnace to heat air that is forced through space consuming ducts and out through registers in the floors.

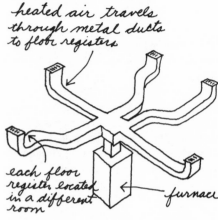

heated air travels through metal ducts to floor registers

each floor register located in a different room

furnace

WARM AIR HEATING SYSTEM

If you can heat a room for $100/year with wood (a 20x20 well-insulated room in N.Y. State), the same room will cost $150/year for kerosene, $300/year for electric, and $250/year for hot water and hot air.

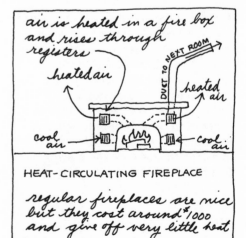

air is heated in a fire box and rises through registers

heated air

DUCT TO NEXT ROOM

heated air

cool air

cool air

HEAT-CIRCULATING FIREPLACE

regular fireplaces are nice but they cost around $1000 and give off very little heat

109

solar heating

As the cost of fossil fuel (oil) goes up, more and more people will be turning to solar heating. The subject is complex and we will only briefly describe the different systems used.

The simplest, least expensive system for heating a space is known as the *Trombe-type air heater,* merely a massive wall facing south, painted black to absorb the sun's rays and placed behind one or more layers of glass. During the day the sun's rays heat the black painted wall. The massive wall stores enough heat to heat the room during the night.

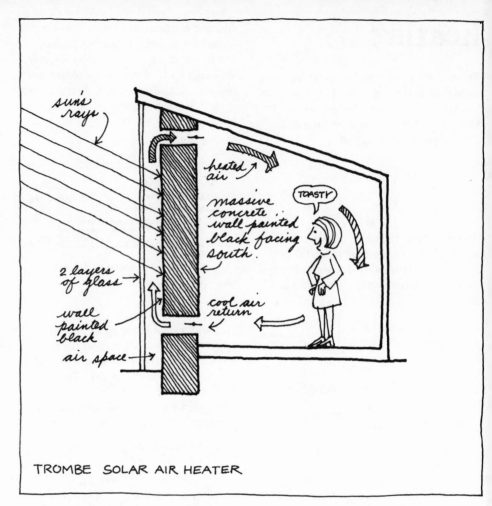

TROMBE SOLAR AIR HEATER

A *thermosyphon* is a very simple device for providing solar-heated hot water. The sun heats water in a solar collector which flows to the insulated storage tank by convection. This causes a slow, continuous circulation down from the bottom of the tank, where the cooler water is, to the collector bottom and then back up again. A 4'x8' collector in a good sun location will give 40 to 50 gallons of hot water per day.

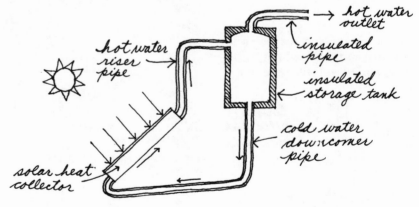

THERMOSYPHON

The most widely used system for solar heating is the *flat plate solar collector.* These flat plates are usually placed on the roof to gather the sun's energy.

There are two basic types of collector systems - air and water. The air system uses air as the medium to gather and transfer heat. It is less expensive than a water system and you don't have to worry about freezing; but it requires more extensive duct work and fans and therefore costs more to run.

The water system uses water as its medium to gather, transfer, and store heat. The primary disadvantage is that water can leak or freeze (usually anti-freeze is added) and eventually corrodes the metal tubes used in the collectors. The air system usually stores heat in a large bin of stones under the house, while the water system uses a large water storage tank. Both air and water systems

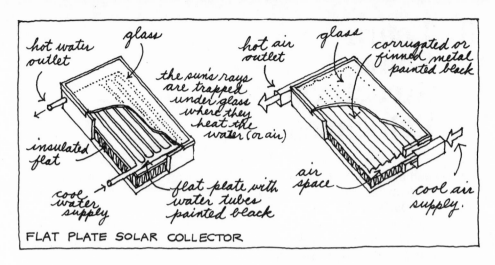

FLAT PLATE SOLAR COLLECTOR

include thermostats and pumps (or fans) to control the heat. There are many variations on these systems.

Shown below are simplified diagrams showing how a solar collector is used with a heat storage tank to heat a house.

The decision to use solar heat should in part be based on climate. In any case, it is generally agreed that you will need a back-up system of some other type of heat for cloudy days. If you are interested in learning more, see the *Energy Primer* (appendix).

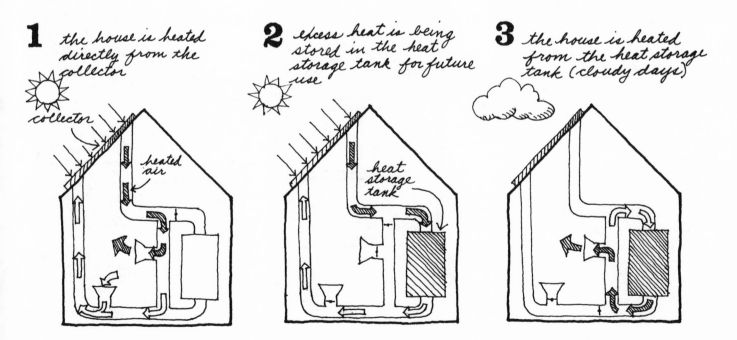

1 the house is heated directly from the collector

2 excess heat is being stored in the heat storage tank for future use

3 the house is heated from the heat storage tank (cloudy days)

3. Learn Some Structural Principles

It is beyond the scope of this book to *fully* explain how to design the structure of a house. But we will describe here the basic principles. Unless you know structure or are following a book on it, you should get some professional advice if you have questions.

A house must be designed to stand up to the forces or loads that will naturally occur. In order to choose what size or type structural materials to use you must know what the *design loads* are.

There are two kinds of loads that must be designed for. *Vertical loads* such as snow and the weight of the building and occupants and *horizontal loads* such as wind and earthquake.

vertical loads

Vertical loads are divided into *live loads* and *dead loads*.

The design for a roof or floor equals the *live load* and the *dead load*.

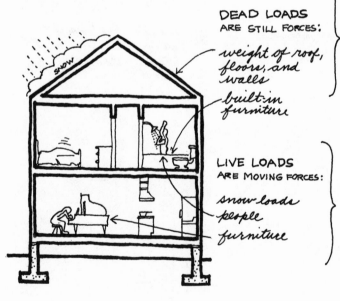

DEAD LOADS ARE STILL FORCES:

weight of roof, floors, and walls

built-in furniture

for a house, a figure of 10 lbs. per sq. ft. is usually used for a dead load.

LIVE LOADS ARE MOVING FORCES:

snow loads
people
furniture

floor live loads are usually figured as 40 lbs. per sq. ft. (except that the 2nd floor and attic can be 30 lbs. per sq. ft.

roof live loads are determined by local snow conditions (20 lbs. per sq. ft. is used as a minimum)

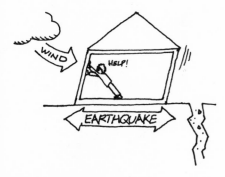

horizontal loads

A house must be braced against the horizontal loads of wind and earthquake. These loads are resisted by the wall sheathing which acts like a rigid diaphragm to prevent deformation (window glass does not count).

The approximate comparative strength of three common wall sheathings are shown below.

WALL TYPE		STRENGTH
	1X8 BOARDS HORIZONTAL NO BRACES	1
	WITH 1X4 LET-IN BRACES	2
	1X8 DIAGONAL SHEATHING	3
	¼" PLYWOOD NAILED	3.5
	NAILED AND GLUED	4

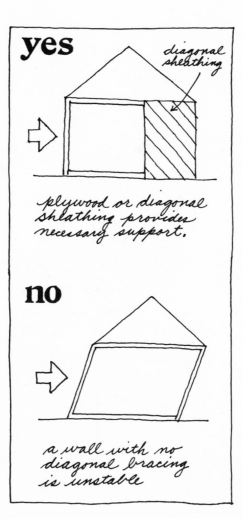

yes

diagonal sheathing

plywood or diagonal shlathing provides necessary support.

no

a wall with no diagonal bracing is unstable

113

sizing a floor or roof joist

The size of a joist can be determined from a span table like the ones in *One and Two Family Dwelling Code.*

To use the span table you need to know 1. the load to be carried, 2. the span of the joist, and 3. the distance between joists. You can then refer to the span table and pick an appropriate joist. This joist will be defined by two engineering figures: *the extreme fiber bending stress* (Fb) and the *modulus of elasticity.* These two figures determine what species and grade of wood must be used. (Each species and grade of wood has a particular ability to span and this is expressed in its Fb and modulus of elasticity.) A listing of the different values can be obtained from *Grading Rules for Western Lumber.* (See appendix.)

If you want to know more about this, a good book is the *Douglas Fir Use Book.* (See appendix.)

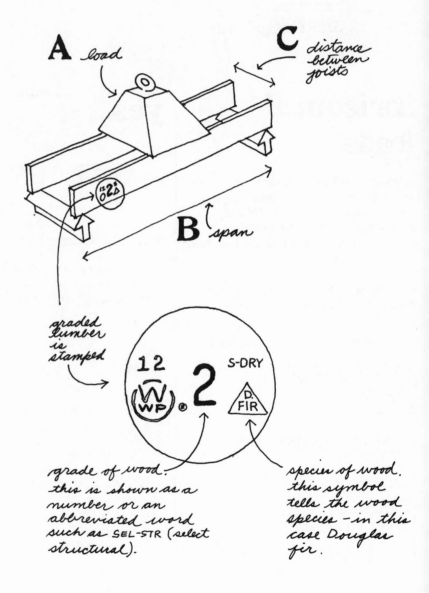

A load

C distance between joists

B span

graded lumber is stamped

12 (W/WP)® 2 S-DRY (D. FIR)

grade of wood.
this is shown as a number or an abbreviated word such as SEL-STR (select structural).

species of wood.
this symbol tells the wood species — in this case Douglas fir.

ONE AND TWO FAMILY DWELLING CODE
(see appendix) good for structure. has span tables for floors and roofs.

114

4. Set Up Your Tools

Here are the tools you'll need to do your construction drawings.

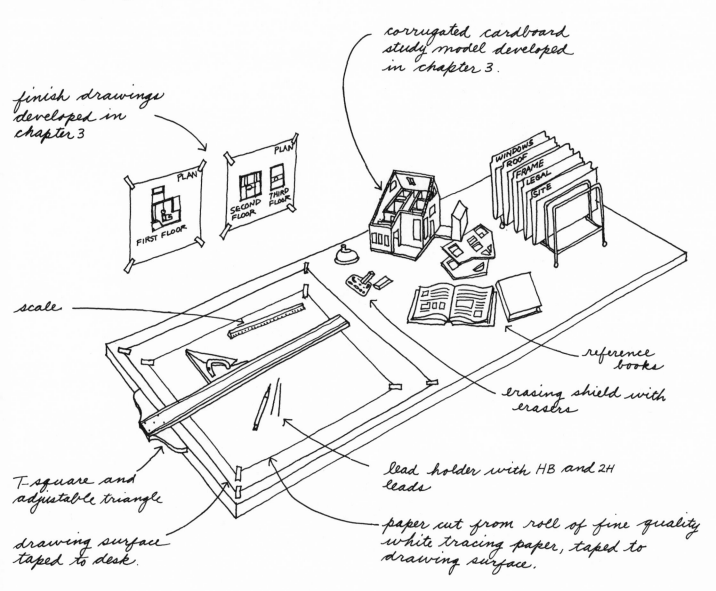

corrugated cardboard study model developed in chapter 3.

finish drawings developed in chapter 3

PLAN

FIRST FLOOR

PLAN

SECOND FLOOR

THIRD FLOOR

WINDOWS
ROOF
FRAME
LEGAL
SITE

scale

reference books

erasing shield with erasers

T-square and adjustable triangle

drawing surface taped to desk.

lead holder with HB and 2H leads

paper cut from roll of fine quality white tracing paper, taped to drawing surface.

5. Lay Out the Sheets

The last task to be done before you start drawing is to determine the sheet or page size, cut the sheets to that size, and roughly lay out the drawings on each sheet.

To determine the sheet size, decide what drawings are necessary to describe your design to the builder. As we mentioned before, most builders need the plans of all floors, one or two sections, all the elevations (N, S, E, and W), and a few sketches. It is best to work this out in thumbnail sketch form first.

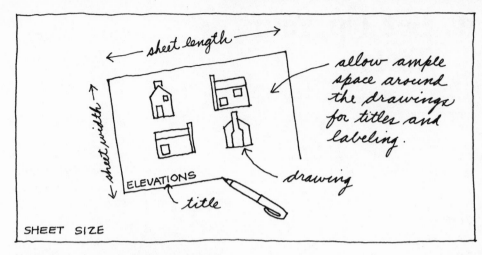

allow ample space around the drawings for titles and labeling.

drawing

title

SHEET SIZE

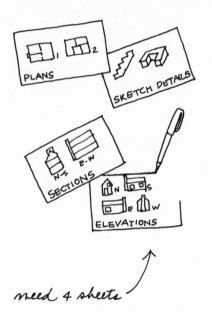

need 4 sheets

Once you've determined the amount of drawings and sheets you need, it is easy to determine the sheet size: using thumbnail sketches again, measure the drawing, allowing ample border space for titles, dimensions, and labels.

Next, cut out the necessary amount of sheets from the roll of good quality tracing paper. Then, lightly pencil in the outline of the drawing that you plan to do on each sheet with your T-square and triangle.

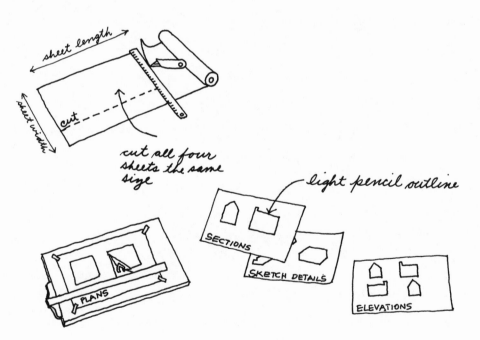

cut all four sheets the same size

light pencil outline

Now you're ready to draw.

C. Drawing

If you can write with a pencil, you can draw well enough to produce a set of drawings suitable for the builder. You don't have to be "good at art", and studying Mechanical Drawing in the eighth grade is not a prerequisite. But patience is, since you will make a few mistakes and a few changes that might snowball into a lot of erasing and re-drawing. But if you follow our step-by-step method, you will find that preparing your own construction drawings is both fun and rewarding.

As you work on your drawing, you will be piecing together graphic symbols (for doors, windows and walls, etc.) into an arrangement that follows your design drawings. Keep in mind that you are only doing the drawing part now. Later you will be dimensioning and labeling this drawing. It is a good idea to practice drawing each of the symbols themselves before you begin your drawing. Most of the symbols you will need are shown next.

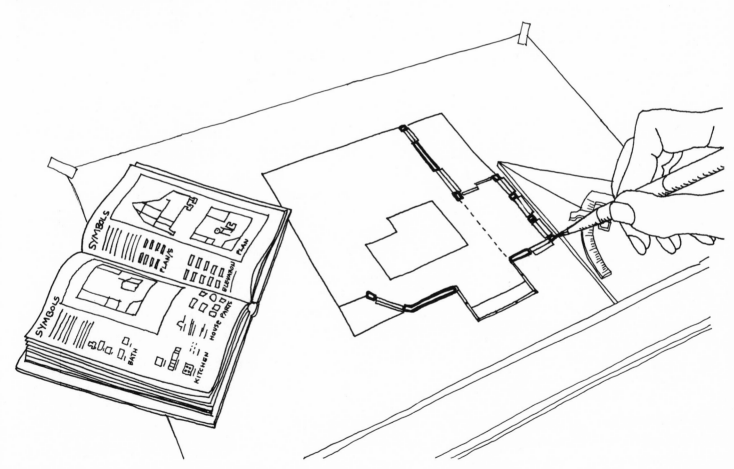

1. Symbols

There are graphic symbols for everything you want to show in your drawing. Architects call these graphic standards. These are standard ways of showing walls, doors, windows, refrigerators, etc. developed by architects and builders to make construction drawings universally understandable. Many of these symbols are shown on page 65 in the design chapter.

Shown here are more detailed symbols for different materials to locate on your drawings. Pick the ones you need from both pages, and draw. You can invent your own as long as your builder understands.

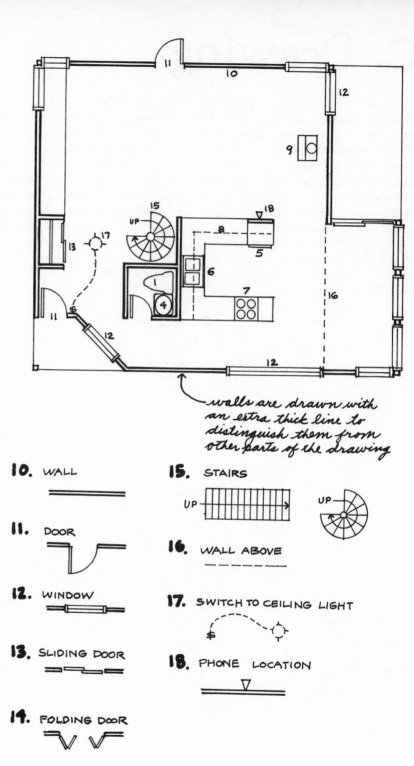

walls are drawn with an extra thick line to distinguish them from other parts of the drawing

plan

1. TOILET

2. TUB

3. SHOWER

4. SINK (*bathroom*)

5. REFRIGERATOR

6. DOUBLE SINK

7. RANGE

8. SHELVING

9. FRANKLIN STOVE

10. WALL

11. DOOR

12. WINDOW

13. SLIDING DOOR

14. FOLDING DOOR

15. STAIRS

UP

UP

16. WALL ABOVE

17. SWITCH TO CEILING LIGHT

$

18. PHONE LOCATION

section

1. CONCRETE BLOCK FOUNDATION

2. WINDOW

3. BRICK WALL

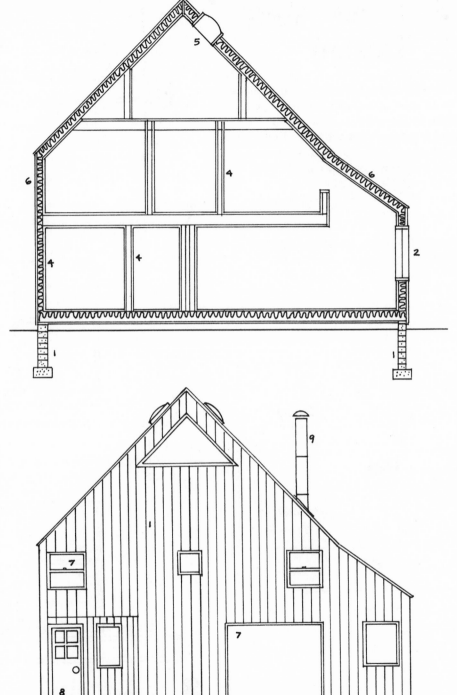

4. STUD WALL *(with inside and outside finish material.)*

5. SKYLIGHT

6. INSULATION

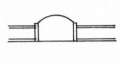

elevation

1. WOOD SIDING

2. WOOD SHINGLES

3. BRICK

4. CONCRETE

5. STONE

6. ASPHALT ROOF SHINGLES.

7. WINDOWS

double hung   *fixed*

8. DOORS

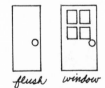

flush   *window*

9. CHIMNEYS

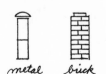

metal   *brick*

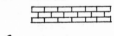

119

2. Draw Your Design

The easiest way to begin your drawing is to outline (with a light pencil line) the basic shape of the drawing and lay out where the windows and doors fit within that shape. Make sure that all the lines you draw, light or heavy, are to scale. (For example, a 4' wide window at ¼" = 1'0" scale would be 1" wide on your drawing.)

Next, fill in the symbols with as much detail as you feel necessary.

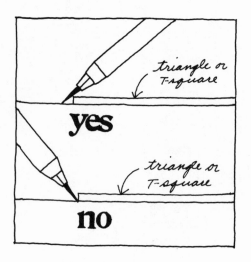

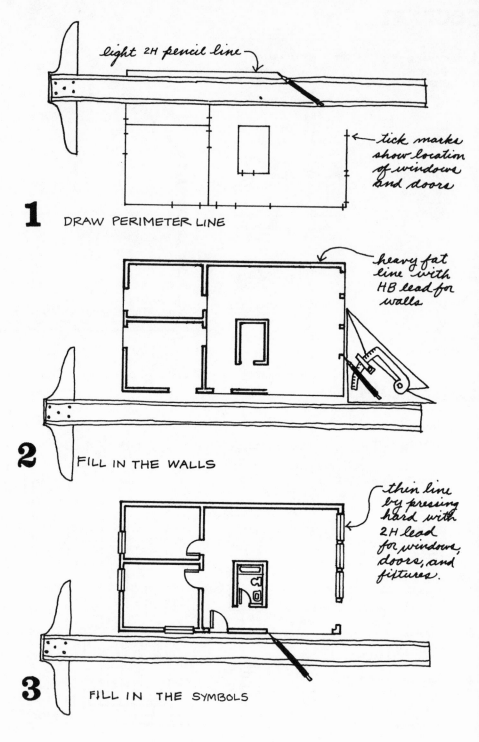

light 2H pencil line

tick marks show location of windows and doors

1 DRAW PERIMETER LINE

heavy fat line with HB lead for walls

2 FILL IN THE WALLS

thin line by pressing hard with 2H lead for windows, doors, and fixtures.

3 FILL IN THE SYMBOLS

triangle or T-square

yes

triangle or T-square

no

And now back to Fred and Lois:
They've been working hard setting themselves up to do their drawings. They've
cleaned up their office and have their
sheets ready to go. They've even had an
argument as to who was to do the actual
drawing - solved when Lois suggested
that she do the plans and sketches while
Fred does the elevations and sections.
They've read the better part of two
books on housebuilding.

But, the most important work they've
accomplished is in their local home improvement center and lumber yards.
Here, they've made decisions on interior and exterior siding, roofing, and
flooring. They choose a hot water heater, bathroom and kitchen sinks, a bath-
tub and two toilets. They pick out an
electric range, a refrigerator, and a
washer-dryer. They spend most of
their time figuring out the best windows for each room, and they get a bro-
chure on greenhouses and one on cabinets and decide to have their carpenter
build custom-designed cabinets rather
than put in factory-made units. They
visit local lighting centers and pick out
some fixtures for kitchen, bath, interior
circulation areas, and the porches.

They decide they are going to do a super
set of drawings and are really excited
about it. They draw a few symbols
with the proper tools, just to get the
hang of it. They dig in and start to
draw.

D. Dimensioning

Dimensioning is the art of showing the builder the sizes of the whole and the parts of your design. It is the easiest yet the most important part of producing your set of drawings. The builder will build according to your dimensions, so if you make a mistake you'll have to live with it.

To show these sizes, architects usually draw a line, with an arrow at each end, parallel to the part they are dimensioning. Then the length of the line is written in, indicating the real length of the part.

OVERALL DIMENSION

If it is necessary to show more detail, usually a second line or "string" of dimensions is added:

This string of dimensions, should always total the same as the first string. Several checks should be made on your dimensions to see that they are accurate.

DETAIL DIMENSION

1. Show the Size of the House

The first information that the builder needs from your drawings is the overall size of the house. This will be your first string of dimensions.

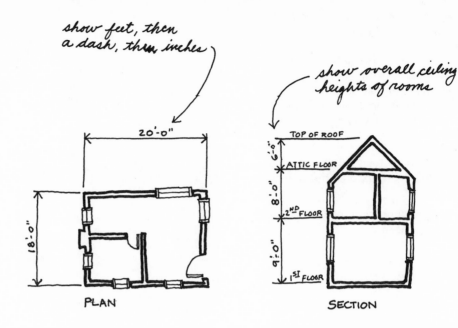

show feet, then a dash, then inches

show overall ceiling heights of rooms

PLAN

SECTION

OVERALL DIMENSION

2. Locate Walls, Doors & Windows

The next step is to draw a second string (or line) of dimensions to locate all the doors, windows and interior walls.

When you dimension any drawing that you make, follow the same general rules: 1. Show an overall dimension. 2. Show a second more detailed string of dimensions.

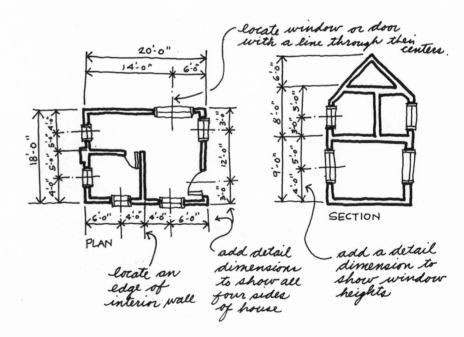

locate window or door with a line through their centers.

locate an edge of interior wall

add detail dimensions to show all four sides of house

add a detail dimension to show window heights

PLAN

SECTION

DETAIL DIMENSION

123

Fred and Lois have completed the "drawing" part of their set of drawings.

Before starting their dimensioning they build a full-scale model from a cardboard box—of built-in storage bins for the kids' bedrooms and of the kitchen cabinets to make sure that they will be "comfortable."

They check all their windows for size by taping their proposed positioning on a blank wall.

Then they dimension the drawings that they have made.

E. Labeling

Labeling is the title we give to notes that describe the materials and important parts of your design. Architects call these notes specifications. They are placed as near to the material or part that you are describing without interfering with the dimension lines or the drawing.

BLUE EYES

YELLOW HAIR

CATALOG #72 RED COTTON DRESS

BROWN FUR

CATALOG #6 BROWN LEATHER SHOES

ELEVATION

LABELING

BUTCHER BLOCK COUNTER TOP

STAINLESS STEEL DOUBLE SINK

CATALOG #123 COOKTOP RANGE

words never touch the drawing

PLAN

Architects usually make light pencil guidelines for all the words about 3/32" apart and print neatly. But, again, we stress that these construction drawings are your means of communication with the builder. If long-hand writing is acceptable with your builder, then it's best.

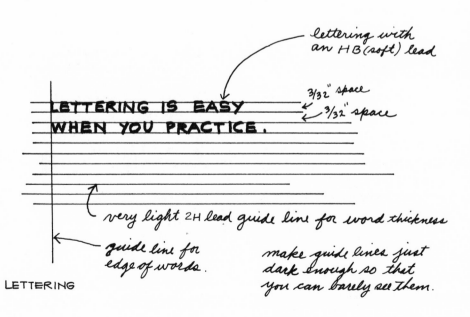

lettering with an HB (soft) lead

LETTERING IS EASY WHEN YOU PRACTICE.

3/32" space

3/32" space

very light 2H lead guide line for word thickness

guide line for edge of words.

make guide lines just dark enough so that you can barely see them.

LETTERING

1. Describe Doors, Windows & Other Important Parts

The easiest way to describe all the various doors and windows in your design is to give each of them a number and make a chart with the numbers listed opposite the necessary information. These charts are called *schedules*.

Windows are usually numbered on the elevations.

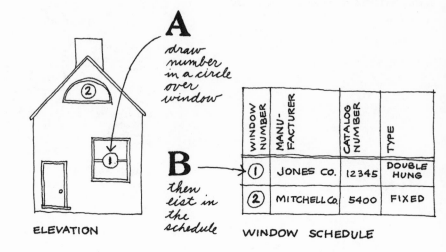

ELEVATION

A draw number in a circle over window

B then list in the schedule

WINDOW SCHEDULE

WINDOW NUMBER	MANU-FACTURER	CATALOG NUMBER	TYPE
①	JONES CO.	12345	DOUBLE HUNG
②	MITCHELL CO.	5400	FIXED

Doors are usually numbered on the plans.

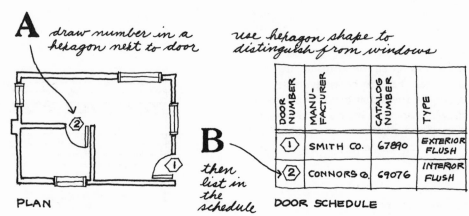

A draw number in a hexagon next to door

use hexagon shape to distinguish from windows

PLAN

B then list in the schedule

DOOR SCHEDULE

DOOR NUMBER	MANU-FACTURER	CATALOG NUMBER	TYPE
⬡1	SMITH CO.	67890	EXTERIOR FLUSH
⬡2	CONNORS CO.	69076	INTERIOR FLUSH

Schedules can be useful for listing plumbing fixtures or other factory-made parts in your design. Just give the part a number in the drawing and then list it separately in a schedule.

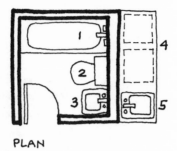

PLAN

FIXTURE NUMBER	MANU- FACTURER	CATALOG NUMBER	FIXTURE
1	SMITH CO.	67	STEEL TUB
2	MITCHELL CO.	96700	TOILET
3	CONNORS CO.	1234	WHITE SINK
4	JONES CO.	3721	WASHER/DRYER
5	SMITH CO.	275	STEEL SINK

FIXTURE SCHEDULE

Usually, however, these important parts are labeled or specified where they appear on your drawing.

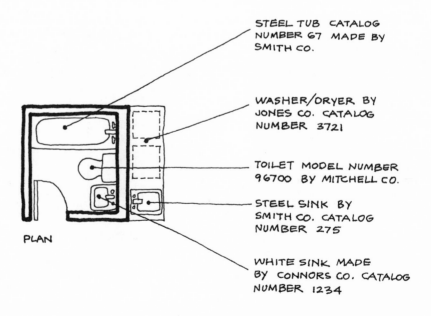

PLAN

STEEL TUB CATALOG NUMBER 67 MADE BY SMITH CO.

WASHER/DRYER BY JONES CO. CATALOG NUMBER 3721

TOILET MODEL NUMBER 96700 BY MITCHELL CO.

STEEL SINK BY SMITH CO. CATALOG NUMBER 275

WHITE SINK MADE BY CONNORS CO. CATALOG NUMBER 1234

2. Specify Siding, Roofing & Other Important Materials

Exterior materials are usually lettered or specified on the elevation drawings - the exterior views of the design. The amount of detail that you get into on these notes again depends on you and your builder. He may require the exact catalog number of the kind of shingle you want on the roof or you may trust him to install what is best for you.

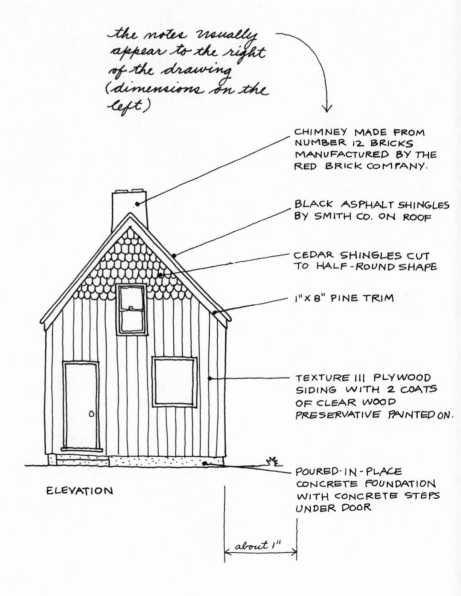

the notes usually appear to the right of the drawing (dimensions on the left)

CHIMNEY MADE FROM NUMBER 12 BRICKS MANUFACTURED BY THE RED BRICK COMPANY.

BLACK ASPHALT SHINGLES BY SMITH CO. ON ROOF

CEDAR SHINGLES CUT TO HALF-ROUND SHAPE

1" X 8" PINE TRIM

TEXTURE III PLYWOOD SIDING WITH 2 COATS OF CLEAR WOOD PRESERVATIVE PAINTED ON.

POURED-IN-PLACE CONCRETE FOUNDATION WITH CONCRETE STEPS UNDER DOOR

ELEVATION

about 1"

128

Interior materials are usually specified with a schedule that lists each room and its six surfaces (ceiling, floor, and four walls), with the vital information about each surface listed in its proper place. This schedule is sometimes known as a finish schedule since it describes the finish in each room.

all of the rooms in the design are listed here

ROOM	CEILING	FLOOR	WALLS			
			NORTH	SOUTH	EAST	WEST
LIVING ROOM						
KITCHEN	PAINTED GYPSUM BOARD	VINYL TILE	ROUGH SAWN PINE	GLASS WINDOW	PAINTED GYPSUM BOARD	PAINTED GYPSUM BOARD
BATH						
BEDROOM						
ENTRY						

FINISH SCHEDULE

the material to be applied to the east wall in the kitchen is listed here.

Don't hesitate to make notes about interior materials directly on the plan drawing or on the sections. This is the simplest way for the builder to read your drawing.

3. Titles

Titles play an important final step in making your set of drawings easy to read. They are used to describe each drawing at a glance so that anyone can leaf through the set and find what they are looking for.

There is a hierarchy of information that titles must convey. This hierarchy extends from the sheet number and general title down to the individual drawing titles. Here is a hierarchy listed from the most visible to the least visible.

These titles should be the most visual, obvious lettering on your sheet. Many architects letter them in ink so that they will stand out from the delicate pencil drawings. The point is to be bold, for clarity's sake.

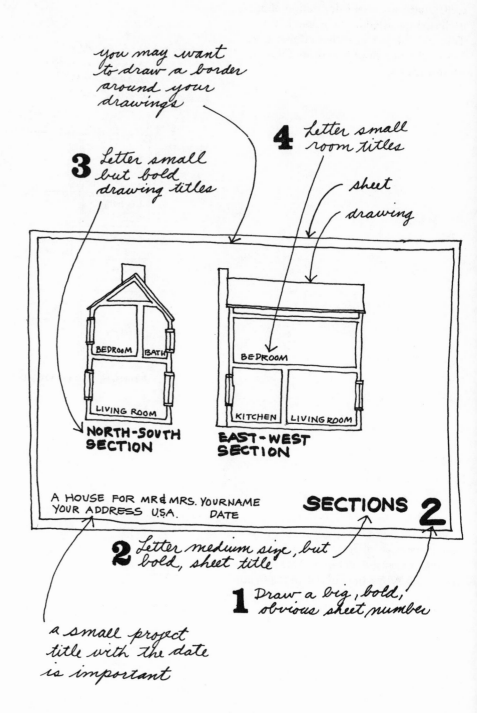

you may want to draw a border around your drawings

3 Letter small but bold drawing titles

4 Letter small room titles

sheet

drawing

BEDROOM BATH

LIVING ROOM

NORTH-SOUTH SECTION

BEDROOM

KITCHEN LIVING ROOM

EAST-WEST SECTION

A HOUSE FOR MR & MRS. YOURNAME
YOUR ADDRESS U.S.A.   DATE

SECTIONS **2**

2 Letter medium size, but bold, sheet title

1 Draw a big, bold, obvious sheet number

a small project title with the date is important

After completing their dimensions, Fred and Lois have another argument about who should do the labeling. They decide to have a lettering contest with their kids as judges.

Phoebe and Jess decide after long deliberation that their father is trying to "show off" with his fancy lettering and so he is "demoted" to doing titles. They think he might enjoy doing the big lettering most.

Lois, with her simple style, wins the competition. She does a great job. And Fred comes through with some nice, clear titles.

The next 12 pages show Fred's and Lois's completed set of construction drawings. They decided against drawing any floor framing plans because their builder said that he didn't need them. But, they did include some first-floor framing information on the foundation plan. They drew an overhanging roof to shade the big living room window on the southwest corner.

Fred's big titles wouldn't fit along the bottom of the pages so he lettered them along the right edge. Lois decided that they didn't need a finish schedule since they were using gypsum board for all the walls and ceilings (except the second floor ceiling) and were going to paint and panel themselves when their budget allowed. So she labeled the interior finish materials on the sections.

Lois was having a very difficult time in drawing her sketch details until Fred suggested that she try using two-point perspective. She did and found that she could explain the kitchen and some built-in furniture by drawing top views.

Fred and Lois are both very proud of their work.

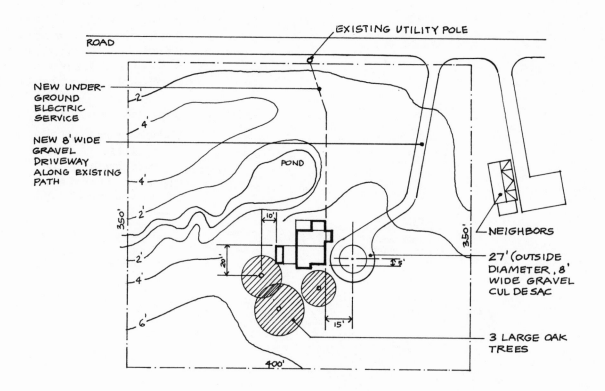

EXISTING UTILITY POLE

ROAD

NEW UNDER-
GROUND
ELECTRIC
SERVICE

NEW 8' WIDE
GRAVEL
DRIVEWAY
ALONG EXISTING
PATH

POND

2'

4'

4'

2'

2'

4'

6'

350'

350'

10'

15'

400'

NEIGHBORS

27' (OUTSIDE
DIAMETER, 8'
WIDE GRAVEL
CUL DE SAC

3 LARGE OAK
TREES

NORTH

site plan

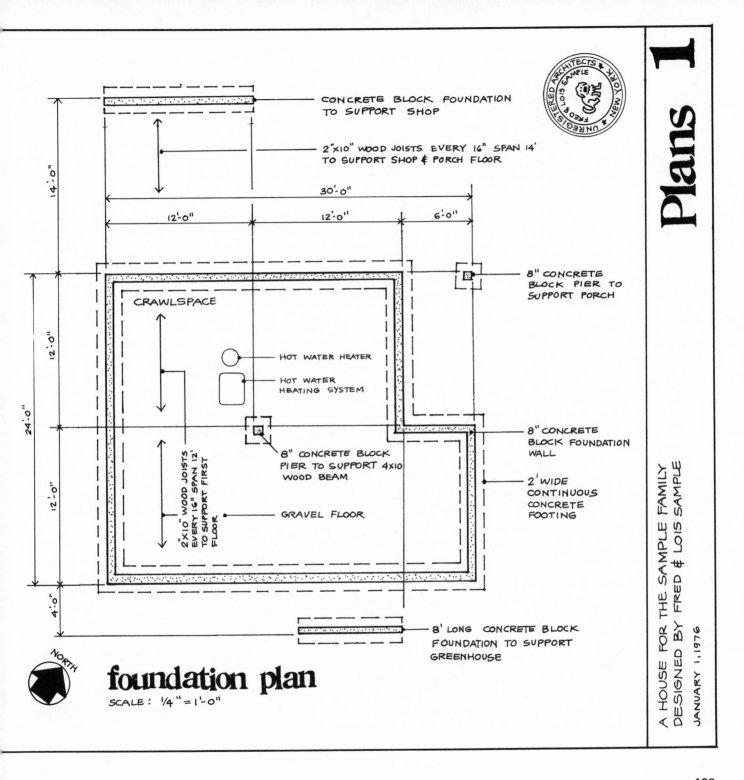

CONCRETE BLOCK FOUNDATION
TO SUPPORT SHOP

2"X10" WOOD JOISTS EVERY 16" SPAN 14'
TO SUPPORT SHOP & PORCH FLOOR

14'-0"

30'-0"

12'-0"   12'-0"   6'-0"

8" CONCRETE
BLOCK PIER TO
SUPPORT PORCH

CRAWLSPACE

12'-0"

24'-0"

HOT WATER HEATER

HOT WATER
HEATING SYSTEM

8" CONCRETE
BLOCK FOUNDATION
WALL

2' WIDE
CONTINUOUS
CONCRETE
FOOTING

8" CONCRETE BLOCK
PIER TO SUPPORT 4x10
WOOD BEAM

2"X10" WOOD JOISTS
EVERY 16" SPAN 12'
TO SUPPORT FIRST
FLOOR

12'-0"

GRAVEL FLOOR

4'-0"

8' LONG CONCRETE BLOCK
FOUNDATION TO SUPPORT
GREENHOUSE

NORTH

foundation plan

SCALE: 1/4" = 1'-0"

A HOUSE FOR THE SAMPLE FAMILY
DESIGNED BY FRED & LOIS SAMPLE

JANUARY 1, 1976

UNREGISTERED ARCHITECTS ★ NEW YORK ★ FRED & LOIS SAMPLE

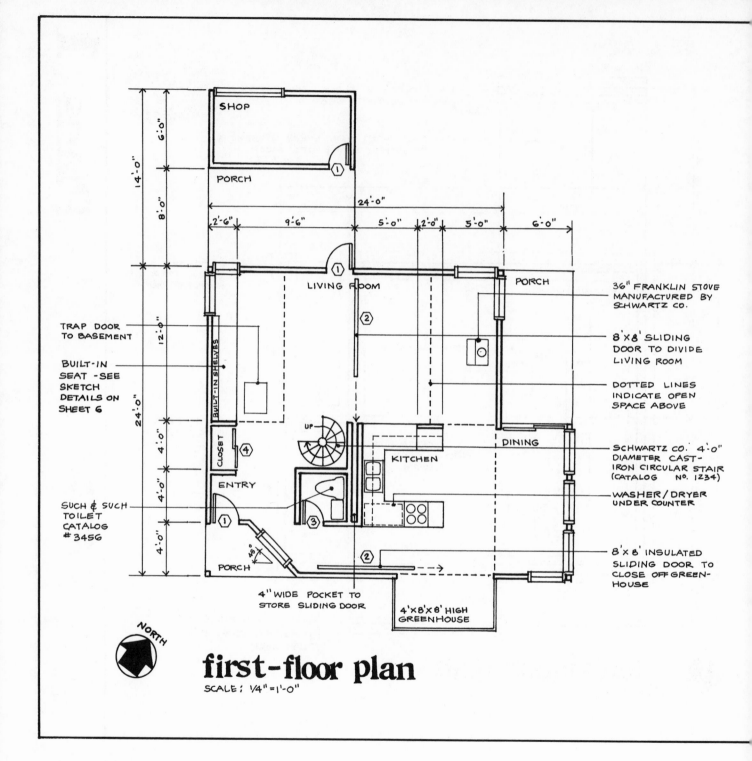

SHOP

PORCH

6'-0"

14'-0"

8'-0"

24'-0"

2'-6" 9'-6" 5'-0" 2'-0" 5'-0" 6'-0"

TRAP DOOR TO BASEMENT

BUILT-IN SEAT -SEE SKETCH DETAILS ON SHEET 6

12'-0"

24'-0"

4'-0"

4'-0"

4'-0"

BUILT-IN SHELVES

CLOSET

ENTRY

SUCH & SUCH TOILET CATALOG #3456

PORCH

45°

LIVING ROOM

UP

KITCHEN

DINING

PORCH

36" FRANKLIN STOVE MANUFACTURED BY SCHWARTZ CO.

8'X8' SLIDING DOOR TO DIVIDE LIVING ROOM

DOTTED LINES INDICATE OPEN SPACE ABOVE

SCHWARTZ CO. 4'-0" DIAMETER CAST-IRON CIRCULAR STAIR (CATALOG NO. 1234)

WASHER/DRYER UNDER COUNTER

8'X8' INSULATED SLIDING DOOR TO CLOSE OFF GREENHOUSE

4" WIDE POCKET TO STORE SLIDING DOOR

4'X8'X8' HIGH GREENHOUSE

NORTH

first-floor plan

SCALE: 1/4"=1'-0"

door schedule

DR #	MANU-FACTURER	CATALOG NUMBER	TYPE
1	JONES CO.	34567	EXTERIOR - WITH WINDOW
2	CONTRACTOR	—	PAINTED T-III PLYWD SLIDING DOOR
3	LEMAIRE CO.	43210	INTERIOR FLUSH
4	CONTRACTOR	—	2'X8' SLIDING ¾" PLYWD. CLOSET DOORS

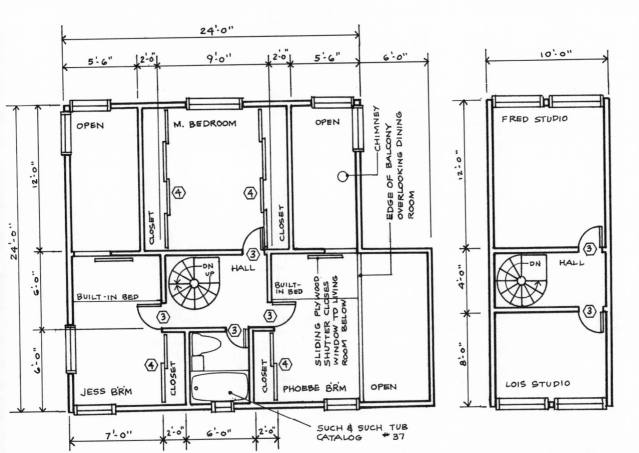

second-floor plan
SCALE: ¼"=1'-0"

third-floor plan
SCALE: ¼"=1'-0"

A HOUSE FOR THE SAMPLE FAMILY
DESIGNED BY FRED & LOIS SAMPLE
JANUARY 1, 1976

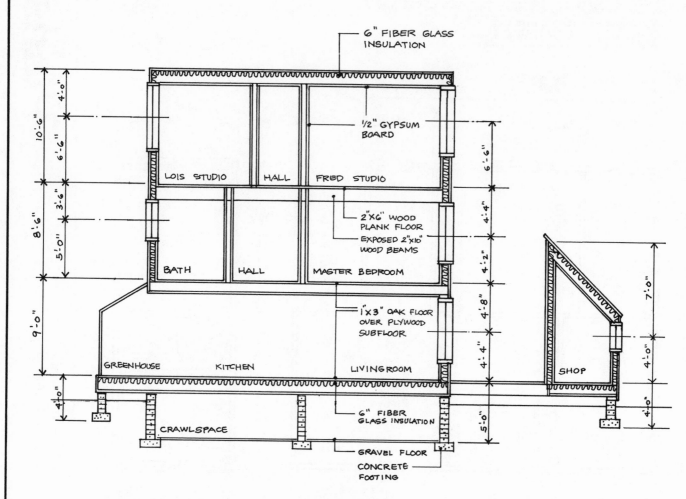

6" FIBER GLASS
INSULATION

1/2" GYPSUM
BOARD

LOIS STUDIO   HALL   FRED STUDIO

2"X6" WOOD
PLANK FLOOR

EXPOSED 2"X10"
WOOD BEAMS

BATH   HALL   MASTER BEDROOM

1"X3" OAK FLOOR
OVER PLYWOOD
SUBFLOOR

GREENHOUSE   KITCHEN   LIVINGROOM   SHOP

6" FIBER
GLASS INSULATION

CRAWLSPACE

GRAVEL FLOOR

CONCRETE
FOOTING

4'-0"   10'-6"   6'-6"   8'-6"   3'-6"   5'-0"   9'-0"   4'-0"
6'-6"   4'-4"   4'-2"   4'-8"   4'-4"   5'-0"   7'-0"   4'-0"

north·south section
SCALE: 1/4" = 1'- 0"

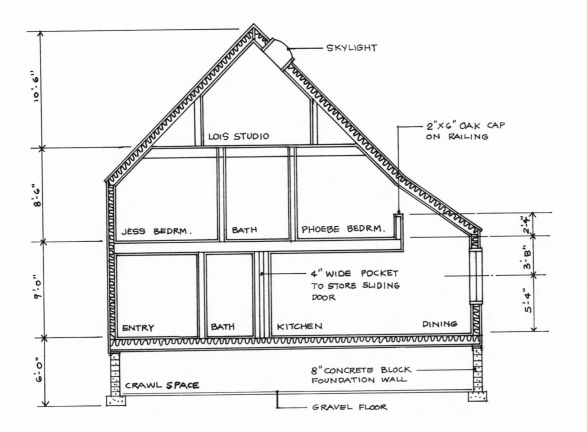

SKYLIGHT

2"×6" OAK CAP
ON RAILING

LOIS STUDIO

JESS BEDRM.   BATH   PHOEBE BEDRM.

4" WIDE POCKET
TO STORE SLIDING
DOOR

ENTRY   BATH   KITCHEN   DINING

8" CONCRETE BLOCK
FOUNDATION WALL

CRAWL SPACE

GRAVEL FLOOR

10'-6"   8'-6"   9'-0"   6'-0"

2'-4"   3'-8"   5'-4"

east · west section

SCALE: ¼"=1'-0"

A HOUSE FOR THE SAMPLE FAMILY
DESIGNED BY FRED & LOIS SAMPLE

JANUARY 1, 1976

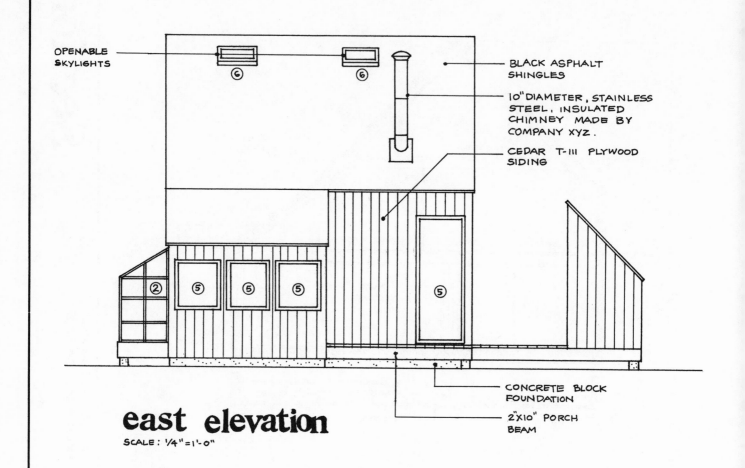

OPENABLE
SKYLIGHTS

BLACK ASPHALT
SHINGLES

10" DIAMETER, STAINLESS
STEEL, INSULATED
CHIMNEY MADE BY
COMPANY XYZ.

CEDAR T-III PLYWOOD
SIDING

CONCRETE BLOCK
FOUNDATION

2"X10" PORCH
BEAM

east elevation

SCALE: 1/4"=1'-0"

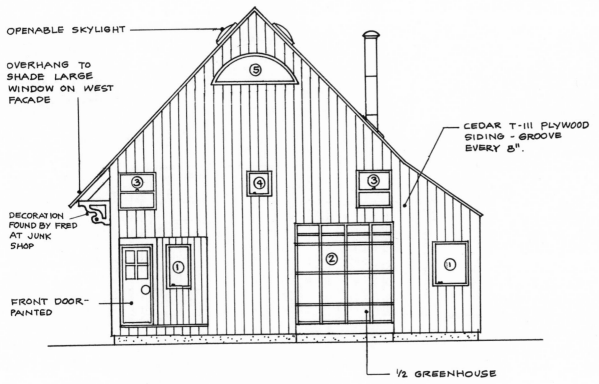

OPENABLE SKYLIGHT

OVERHANG TO
SHADE LARGE
WINDOW ON WEST
FACADE

DECORATION
FOUND BY FRED
AT JUNK
SHOP

FRONT DOOR-
PAINTED

CEDAR T-III PLYWOOD
SIDING - GROOVE
EVERY 8".

½ GREENHOUSE

south elevation

SCALE : ¼" = 1'-0"

A HOUSE FOR THE SAMPLE FAMILY
DESIGNED BY FRED & LOIS SAMPLE

JANUARY 1, 1976

139

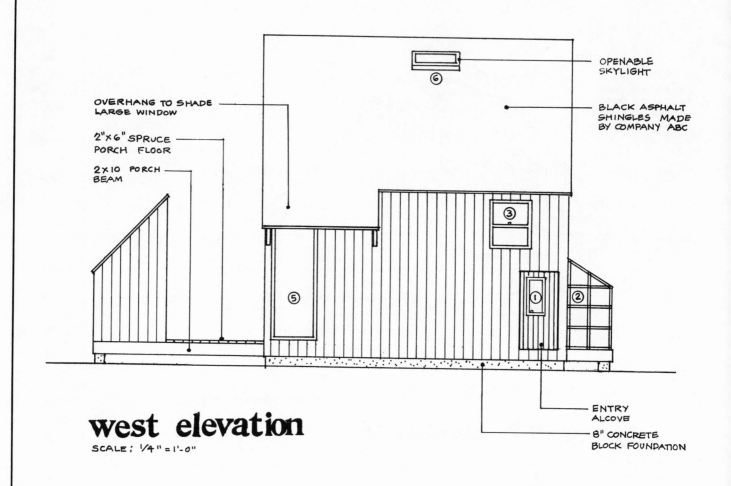

OPENABLE
SKYLIGHT

BLACK ASPHALT
SHINGLES MADE
BY COMPANY ABC

OVERHANG TO SHADE
LARGE WINDOW

2"×6" SPRUCE
PORCH FLOOR

2×10 PORCH
BEAM

ENTRY
ALCOVE

8" CONCRETE
BLOCK FOUNDATION

west elevation

SCALE: 1/4" = 1'-0"

window schedule

WDW. #	MANU-FACTURER	CATALOG NUMBER	TYPE
①	JONES CO.	1234	CASEMENT
②	ACTION CO.	3473	½ GREENHOUSE
③	JONES CO.	2132	DOUBLE HUNG
④	JONES CO.	2147	CASEMENT
⑤	CONTRACTOR	—	FIXED
⑥	NIVIN CO.	3728	SKYLIGHT
⑦	JONES CO.	1752	COMBINATION

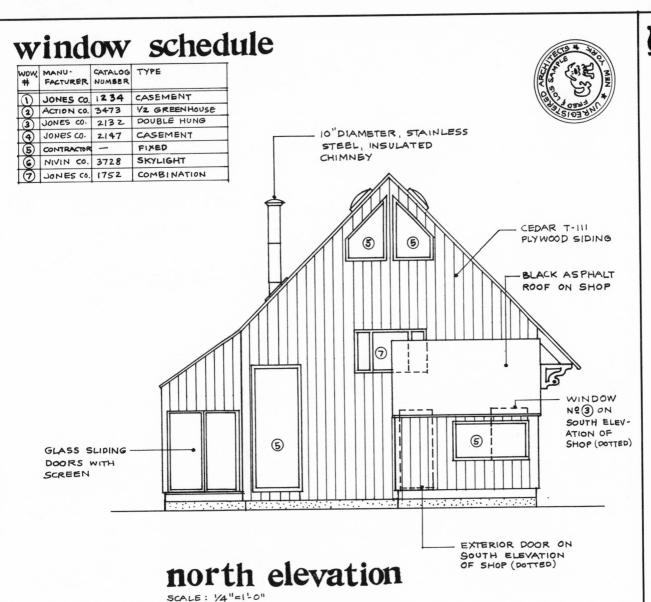

10" DIAMETER, STAINLESS STEEL, INSULATED CHIMNEY

CEDAR T-111 PLYWOOD SIDING

BLACK ASPHALT ROOF ON SHOP

WINDOW N° ③ ON SOUTH ELEVATION OF SHOP (DOTTED)

GLASS SLIDING DOORS WITH SCREEN

EXTERIOR DOOR ON SOUTH ELEVATION OF SHOP (DOTTED)

north elevation

SCALE: ¼" = 1'-0"

A HOUSE FOR THE SAMPLE FAMILY DESIGNED BY FRED & LOIS SAMPLE

JANUARY 1, 1976

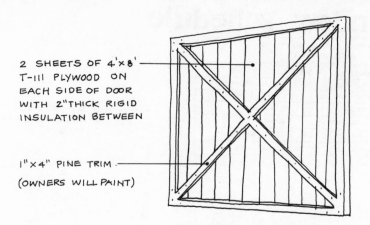

2 SHEETS OF 4'x 8'
T-111 PLYWOOD ON
EACH SIDE OF DOOR
WITH 2" THICK RIGID
INSULATION BETWEEN

1"x 4" PINE TRIM

(OWNERS WILL PAINT)

sliding door

MAKE 2: 1 FOR LIVING ROOM
AND 1 FOR GREENHOUSE

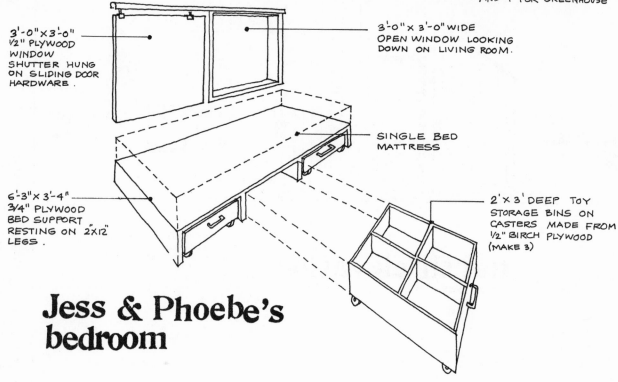

3'-0" x 3'-0"
1/2" PLYWOOD
WINDOW
SHUTTER HUNG
ON SLIDING DOOR
HARDWARE.

3'-0" x 3'-0" WIDE
OPEN WINDOW LOOKING
DOWN ON LIVING ROOM.

SINGLE BED
MATTRESS

6'-3" x 3'-4"
3/4" PLYWOOD
BED SUPPORT
RESTING ON 2"x12"
LEGS.

2' x 3' DEEP TOY
STORAGE BINS ON
CASTERS MADE FROM
1/2" BIRCH PLYWOOD
(MAKE 3)

Jess & Phoebe's bedroom

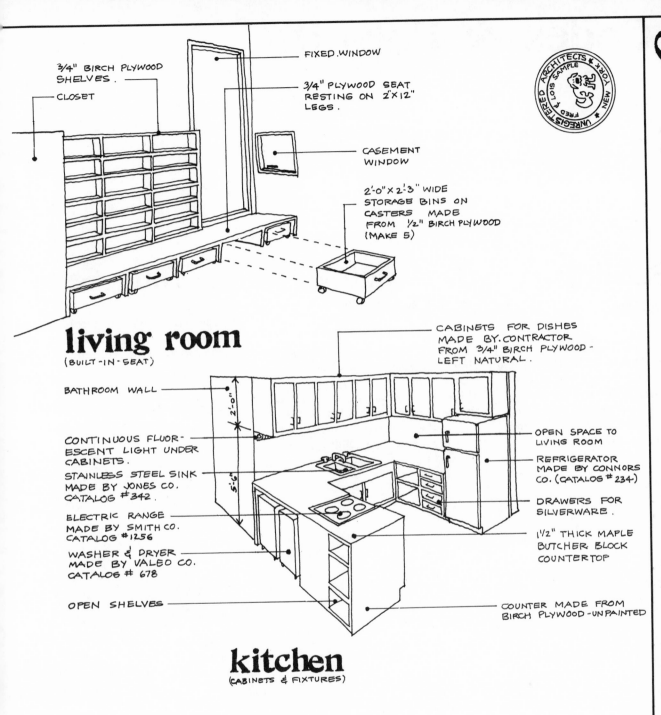

3/4" BIRCH PLYWOOD SHELVES.

CLOSET

FIXED WINDOW

3/4" PLYWOOD SEAT RESTING ON 2"x12" LEGS.

CASEMENT WINDOW

2'-0" X 2'-3" WIDE STORAGE BINS ON CASTERS MADE FROM 1/2" BIRCH PLYWOOD (MAKE 5)

living room
(BUILT-IN-SEAT)

CABINETS FOR DISHES MADE BY CONTRACTOR FROM 3/4" BIRCH PLYWOOD - LEFT NATURAL.

BATHROOM WALL

2'-0"

CONTINUOUS FLUOR-ESCENT LIGHT UNDER CABINETS.

STAINLESS STEEL SINK MADE BY JONES CO. CATALOG #342.

5'-6"

ELECTRIC RANGE MADE BY SMITH CO. CATALOG #1256

WASHER & DRYER MADE BY VALEO CO. CATALOG # 678

OPEN SHELVES

OPEN SPACE TO LIVING ROOM

REFRIGERATOR MADE BY CONNORS CO. (CATALOG #234)

DRAWERS FOR SILVERWARE.

1 1/2" THICK MAPLE BUTCHER BLOCK COUNTERTOP

COUNTER MADE FROM BIRCH PLYWOOD - UNPAINTED

kitchen
(CABINETS & FIXTURES)

A HOUSE FOR THE SAMPLE FAMILY
DESIGNED BY FRED & LOIS SAMPLE

JANUARY 1, 1976

UNREGISTERED FRED & LOIS SAMPLE ARCHITECTS NEW YORK

F. Codes & Permits

1. Building Codes

There are many different building codes, or laws, covering everything from zoning to plumbing. Different localities have different codes (some have no codes). You must find out what codes are applicable where you intend to build and become familiar with them.

2. Building Permit

In many communities, in order to build your home you must first obtain permission from the Building Inspector. This is done by filing a formal application with your drawings for the future house. If your design satisfies all local code requirements, a building permit is issued.

3. Your Seal

Now here is an unofficial architect's seal to trace on all your sheets near the sheet number so that it can be easily seen.

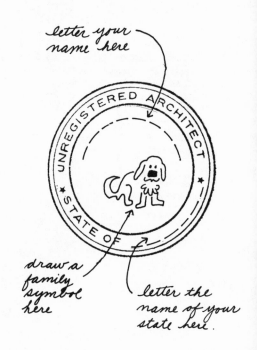

letter your name here

draw a family symbol here

letter the name of your state here.

G. Construction Contracts and Supervision

No matter how much you and your contractor like each other, you should put in writing what each expects from the other. List any items not specifically shown on the drawings that you expect the contractor to do. Be sure to include a period of time during which you expect the house to be built. The amount and method of payment should be stated.

There are two usual forms of payment. One is a fixed bid for which the contractor agrees to provide everything shown in the drawings for one sum, stated before construction begins. The second method is where the contractor charges for his materials and an hourly amount to cover labor and overhead.

The actual payment to the contractor is generally made in three or four installments, each to cover the work done up to the time of billing.

This is one reason why it is important to supervise the construction: to see that the work being billed for was actually done. The second reason is to see that the drawings are followed without error or substitution. It is important to realize that no matter how good your drawings are they will not be complete, and the contractor will have to make many decisions on his own. Therefore, it is necessary to have a certain amount of trust between you and the contractor. There will be times when he will want to change or substitute, and you must use your judgment.

145

Fred and Lois get four sets of prints made by a blueprinter in their town, listed under "printing" in the Yellow Pages. They keep one set for themselves, use one set to file with the building inspector (after making a few minor changes required by him), and give two sets to the builder. They keep their original drawings in case more sets of prints are needed.

These sets of prints represent a great deal of time and energy but now Fred and Lois can relax. They walk down to their empty building site, with the sun setting, a little mist on the pond. The feeling that a building of their design is soon to be erected is exciting. They are going to live happily ever after in their own "architect-designed" home.

Appendix 1

Reference Books

Architectural Graphic Standards
Ramsey & Sleeper, John Wiley & Sons
Publishing Co., 1530 So. Redwood Rd.,
Salt Lake City, Utah. $39.50
*A big expensive book. Very good for
drawing reference.*

Douglas Fir Use Book
West Coast Lumbermans Assoc., 1410
S.W. Morrison St., Portland, Ore.
$5.00
*A good reference book on how to en-
gineer wood buildings.*

Energy Primer
Portola Institute, 558 Santa Cruz Ave.,
Menlo Park, Calif. 94025 $4.50
*A comprehensive reference book on alter-
nate forms of energy: solar, water, wind
and biofuels.*

Illustrated Housebuilding
Monk Blackburne, Overlook Press, Lewis
Hollow Road, Woodstock, New York.
$10.00
*An excellent book on building a wood-
frame house.*

Modern Carpentry
Willis H. Wagner, Goodheart-Willcox Co.,
Inc., South Holland, Ill.
*A good book on housebuilding tech-
niques with lots of pictures.*

One and Two Family Dwelling Code
International Conference of Building
Officials, 50 South Los Robles, Pasadena,
Calif.
*A good general code reference contain-
ing span tables for floors and roofs.*

The Owner Built Home
Ken Kern, Ken Kern Drafting, Sierra
Route, Oakhurst, Calif. 93644. $5.00
*A good building and design reference
that includes many unusual building
methods.*

Shelter
Shelter Publications, Mountain Books,
P.O. Box 4811, Santa Barbara, Calif.
93103. $6.00 + .60 handling.
*A rich "Whole Earth Catalog" type
source of building ideas.*

Grading Rules for Western Lumber
Western Wood Products Association,
1500 Yeon Building, Portland, Ore.
97204
*A guide to determining the allowable
stresses in different species of wood.*

Magazines

Abitare
Via Guerrazzi 1
20145 Milano, Italy
$25/yr. for 12 issues (approximate)
*The best of the European home maga-
zines containing hundreds of exciting
ideas in each issue.*

Architectural Record Houses
1221 Avenue of Americas, N.Y., N.Y.
10020
*A once-a-year publication of award-win-
ning houses (mostly expensive).*

Popular Science
P.O. Box 2871, Boulder, Colo. 80302.
$6.94/yr. for 12 issues.
*The best of the home improvement
service magazines containing many interesting do-it-yourself ideas.*

Progressive Architecture
Industrial Publishing Co., 614 Superior
Ave., West Cleveland, Ohio 44113
*A good architectural journal that re-
ports on the profession in America.*

Appendix 2

Supplies

Charrette Co.
2000 Massachusetts Ave., Cambridge,
Mass. 02140
*They sell drafting supplies, have dis-
counts, and will send you a free catalog.*

R.A. Stewart Co.
85 White St., N.Y., N.Y. 10013
*They sell sign markers and will send
you a free catalog.*

Cost of sign markers:

1/4" high letters and numbers	*no. 914*	*$13.00*
3/8" high letters and numbers	*no. 916*	*$14.80*
1/2" high letters and numbers	*no. 918*	*$15.40*

Appendix 3

If you ever need help with any part of your work, visit one of the architectural schools listed below and hunt down an energetic student.

If you can't get the kind of help you need, don't hesitate to ask a local architect, engineer, or builder.

Arizona, University of
Tucson, Arizona 85721
College of Architecture
(602) 884-3134

Arizona State University
Tempe, Arizona 85281
College of Architecture
(602) 965-3216

Arkansas, University of
Fayetteville, Ark. 72701
Department of Architecture
(501) 575-4705

Auburn University
Auburn, Ala. 36830
School of Architecture and Fine Arts
(205) 826-4524

Ball State University
Muncie, Indiana 47306
College of Architecture and Planning
(317) 285-4481

Boston Architectural Center
Boston, Massachusetts 02115
(617) 536-3170

California, University of
Berkeley, Calif. 94720
Department of Architecture,
College of Environmental Design
(415) 642-4942

California Polytechnic State University
San Luis Obispo, Calif. 93401
School of Architecture and Environmental Design
(805) 526-2497

Carnegie-Melon University
Pittsburgh, Pa. 15213
Department of Architecture
(412) 621-2600

Catholic University of America
Washington, D.C. 20017
Department of Architecture and Planning
(202) 529-6000

Cincinnati, University of
Cincinnati, Ohio 45221
College of Design, Architecture and Art
(513) 475-2842

The City College of the City University of N.Y.
New York, N.Y. 10031
School of Architecture
(212) 621-2118

Clemson University
Clemson, S.C. 29631
College of Architecture
(803) 656-3081

Colorado, University of
Boulder, Colorado 80302
College of Environmental Design
(303) 443-2211 x7711

Columbia University
New York, N.Y. 10027
Graduate School of Architecture and Planning
(212) 280-3504

Cooper Union
New York, N.Y. 10003
Division of Architecture
(212) 254-6300

Cornell University
Ithaca, N.Y. 14850
College of Architecture, Art and Planning
(607) 256-4912

Detroit, University
Detroit, Mich. 48221
School of Architecture and Environmental Studies
(313) 342-1000 x532

Drexel University
Evening College
Philadelphia, Pa. 19104
Department of Architecture
(215) 895-2160

Florida, University of
Gainesville, Fla. 32601
Department of Architecture
(904) 392-0204

Georgia Institute of Technology
Atlanta, Ga. 30332
School of Architecture
(404) 894-4885

Hampton Institute
Hampton, Virginia 23368
Department of Architecture
(703) 727-5440 x5441

Harvard University
Cambridge, Mass. 02138
Graduate School of Design
(617) 495-2568

University of Hawaii
Honolulu, Hawaii 96822
Department of Architecture
(808) 948-7225

Houston, University of
Houston, Texas 77004
College of Architecture
(713) 749-1188

Howard University
Washington, D.C. 20001
School of Architecture and Planning
(202) 636-7420

Idaho, University of
Moscow, Idaho 83843
Department of Art and Architecture
(208) 885-6272

Illinois Institute of Technology
Chicago, Ill. 60616
School of Architecture and Planning
(312) 225-9600 x468

Illinois, University of
Chicago Circle
Chicago, Ill. 60680
Department of Architecture
(312) 996-3335

Illinois, University of
Urbana, Ill. 61801
Department of Architecture
(217) 333-1330

Iowa State University
Ames, Iowa 50010
Department of Architecture
(515) 294-4718

Kansas State University
Manhattan, Kansas 66502
College of Architecture and Design
(913) 532-5950

Kansas, University of
Lawrence, Kansas 66044
School of Architecture and Urban Design
(913) 864-4281

Kent State University
Kent, Ohio 44242
School of Architecture
(216) 672-2917

Kentucky, University of
Lexington, Ky. 40506
College of Architecture
(606) 258-5771

Louisiana State University
Baton Rouge, La. 70803
Department of Architecture
(504) 388-2821

Maryland, University of
College Park, Maryland 20742
School of Architecture
(301) 454-5168

Massachusetts Institute of Technology
Cambridge, Mass. 02139
Department of Architecture
(617) 263-4411

Miami, University of
Oxford, Ohio 45056
Department of Architecture
(513) 529-6426

Michigan, University of
Ann Arbor, Michigan 48104
College of Architecture and Design
Department of Architecture
(313) 764-1315

Minnesota, University of
Minneapolis, Minn. 55455
School of Architecture and Landscape
Architecture
(612) 373-2851

Montana State University
Bozeman, Mont. 59715
School of Architecture
(406) 994-4255

Nebraska, University of
Lincoln, Nebr. 68508
College of Architecture
(402) 472-3553

New Mexico, University of
Albuquerque, N.M. 87106
Department of Architecture
(505) 277-2903

North Carolina State University
Raleigh, N.C. 27607
Department of Architecture
(919) 737-2204

North Dakota State University
Fargo, North Dakota 58102
Department of Architecture
(701) 237-7868

Notre Dame, University of
Notre Dame, Indiana 46556
Department of Architecture
(219) 283-6137

Ohio State University
Columbus, Ohio 43210
School of Architecture
(614) 422-6806

Oklahoma State University
Stillwater, Okla. 74074
School of Architecture
(405) 372-6211 x7567

Oklahoma, University of
Norman, Okla. 73069
School of Architecture
(405) 325-2444

Oregon, University of
Eugene, Ore. 97403
School of Architecture and Allied Arts
Department of Architecture
(503) 686-3657

Pennsylvania, University of
Philadelphia, Pa. 19174
Graduate School of Fine Arts
(215) 594-8321

Pennsylvania State University
University Park, Pa. 16802
Division of Environmental Design and
Planning, Dept. of Architecture
(814) 865-9535

Pratt Institute
Brooklyn, N.Y. 11205
School of Architecture
(212) 622-2200

Princeton University
Princeton, N.J. 08540
School of Architecture and Urban
Planning
(609) 452-3737

Puerto Rico, University of
San Juan, Puerto Rico 00931
School of Architecture
(809) 765-9935

Rensselaer Polytechnic Institute
Troy, N.Y. 12181
School of Architecture
(518) 270-6460

Rhode Island School of Design
Providence, R.I. 02903
Division of Architectural Studies
(401) 331-3507

Rice University
Houston, Texas 77001
School of Architecture
(713) 528-4141 x252

Southern University
Baton Rouge, Louisiana 70813
Department of Architecture
(504) 771-5291

Southern California, University of
Los Angeles, Calif. 90007
School of Architecture and Fine Arts
(213) 746-2725

Southwestern Louisiana, University of
Lafayette, Louisiana 70501
School of Art and Architecture
Architecture Section
(318) 233-3850

Syracuse University
Syracuse, N.Y. 13210
School of Architecture
(315) 423-2255

Tennessee, University of
Knoxville, Tenn. 37916
School of Architecture
(615) 974-5265

Texas A&M University
College Station, Texas 77843
College of Architecture and Environmental Design
(713) 845-1221

Texas Tech University
Lubbock, Texas 79409
Department of Architecture
(806) 743-3136

Texas, University of
Austin, Texas 78712
School of Architecture
(512) 471-1992

Tulane University
New Orleans, La. 70118
School of Architecture
(504) 865-6472

Tuskegee Institute
Tuskegee Institute, Ala. 36088
Department of Architecture
(205) 727-8330 or 8329

Utah, University of
Salt Lake City, Utah 84112
Department of Architecture
(801) 8254

Virginia Polytechnic Institute & State
University
Blacksburg, Va. 24061
College of Architecture
(703) 552-6415

Virginia, University of
Charlottesville, Va. 22903
School of Architecture
(703) 924-7019

Washington University
St. Louis, Mo. 63130
School of Architecture
(314) 863-0100

Washington, University of
Seattle, Wash. 98105
College of Architecture and Urban Planning
Department of Architecture
(206) 543-4180

Washington State University
Pullman, Wash. 99163
Department of Architecture
College of Engineering
(509) 335-5539

Yale University
New Haven, Conn. 06520
School of Architecture
(203) 436-0550

the end